RESTORATION

First published by Charco Press 2025
Charco Press Ltd., Office 59, 44-46 Morningside Road, Edinburgh
EH10 4BF

A CIP catalogue record for this book is available from the British Library.

ISBN: 9781917260022
e-book: 9781917260039

www.charcopress.com

Edited by Fionn Petch
Cover designed by Pablo Font
Typeset by Laura Jones-Rivera
Proofread by Fiona Mackintosh

EU GPSR Authorised Representative
LOGOS EUROPE, 9 rue Nicolas Poussin,
17000, LA ROCHELLE, France
E-mail: Contact@logoseurope.eu

2 4 6 8 10 9 7 5 3 1

Ave Barrera

RESTORATION

Translated by
Robin Myers and Ellen Jones

CHARCO ◭ PRESS

For Janet Mérida

In memory of Lara Barrera

Perhaps I am a remote memory in the mind of someone else whom I have imagined myself to be…

I am the materialization of something that is at the point of evaporating, a memory at the point of being forgotten…

Farabeuf, Salvador Elizondo

(trans. by John Incledon)

ONE

REMEMBER?

The photograph shows a body being dismembered. The face looks up at the sky as if in a trance, beyond pain. I recognise it. It's my face. I unstick the photo from the board. Hold the corner of the paper between my forefinger and thumb. Breathe. I feel my pulse pounding. It's me. The body mounted on the three-legged structure is my body, naked, completely exposed; arms tied behind the back, collarbones straining white against the skin. Blood trickles down the torso from the amputated breasts to the pubis. Of the legs, the image shows only what's left of the thighs. The pale skin stands out against the black cloth covering the floor and wall behind. I'm that scrap of light, undeniable synecdoche for a reality that has vanished from my memory. I look at my body, this other one, the present one, clothed, intact; standing at the cork board, detached from itself. Like when you look into a triptych mirror and recognise the image, but as something different and unsettling, more real.

Two men also appear in the image. They stand behind me, holding the posts. Their faces are hidden by the shadow or the angle. The portly one wears a lab coat and holds a medical saw. The other one, the dignitary, wears a tweed jacket. Both stretch their arms towards the body, consciously forming the shape of the Chinese ideogram *liu*. A third man takes the photo, pressing the shutter at just the right moment.

I remember the first time Zuri showed me the house. He took my hand as we crossed the street, stopped on the corner, then said suddenly: This is it. I looked up at the neo-colonial façade. It was a three-storey mansion surrendered to the embrace of dead vines. My eyes travelled over the cool heights of the walls, the finish of the pink cantera stone carved into scrolls and bouquets, set against a smooth white backdrop riven with cracks and stains where the rain had run. The top of a tulip tree caressed the roof and the arches on the highest turret. Sunlight sifted through the branches. Threadbare curtains offered glimpses of shadows and neglect.

Ever since I was a girl, whenever I pass a house like this, I've been overcome by a strange desire to rescue it from abandonment; an urge to walk across its gleaming, wax-scented floors, to dream under those high ceilings and take in the cool afternoon breeze as I lean against a balcony. I wish I lived there, I'd think, unbidden, whenever I saw a ruined, wasted palace from the outside. I longed to tell the neglectful owners I'd happily wax the floors, fill the flowerpots, shoo away the silence with music from old *chanson française* records, warm the reception rooms with the crackle of fire and the smell of freshly baked bread.

We stood at the metal gate on the corner while Zuri rummaged around in his rucksack for the keys. I went over to the enclosing stone wall. Each section had an inset clay lattice of half-moons, patterned like fish scales. Through the gaps I could see a footpath extending all the way around the building, like the moat of a mediaeval castle. I reached out to stroke the moss that had grown over the clay. Zuri pulled out the bunch of keys and tried the first. He seemed nervous.

I, on the other hand, felt relieved, glad things were getting back to normal. The past few days had been hell on earth for me. We'd argued and he'd left without a word. It wasn't the first time − he'd disappear for a few days, then suddenly show up at the Institute, take me out for an ice cream and tell me he'd been having one of his crises. He'd ask me to understand, to be patient. But this time was different: not only because of the argument, but also because three whole weeks had gone by without any sign of him. I'd sent him all manner of messages: desperate, conciliatory, affectionate, concerned, angry. And as if the confusion weren't enough, I realised my period was late.

I was beginning to wonder whether I might never see him again when his call came − same as always, no hello, no goodbye, no niceties. Breakfast tomorrow? he asked, as though it was any other Friday at 6.40 pm. I hesitated. I wanted to ask if he was alright, if we were alright, but I knew his immediate reaction would be to hang up, so I said: Yes, see you tomorrow. And he hung up. I could barely sleep for agonising over what to say, how to act. So I was enormously cheered when he arrived and hugged me as though nothing had happened. He buried his face in my neck, breathed deeply, and I felt him smile. Then we pulled apart, went into the restaurant, sat down in the second booth by the window, turned over our cups and waited for them to bring the jug of coffee. Like every Saturday, he ordered eggs Benedict, toast, grapefruit juice and rhubarb tart. It was chilaquiles rojos for me this time.

When the waitress had taken our order, Zuri began to talk about his trip to Chicago as though I was already up to date and all he had to do was fill in the details. He told me about the nights he'd spent at the hospital at his great uncle's bedside, about how hard he'd found it, restless, unable to sleep, exposed to possible infection. He talked about the perpetual smell of sour milk in his aunt Silvia's house, where he'd been staying. On the third day, Don Eligio went into respiratory arrest, and what followed felt like a murky dream: his death, the paperwork, the poorly attended funeral, the reading of the will, the wish for his ashes to be scattered at the old family home, abandoned for more than thirty years.

It all felt so light-hearted and amicable that for a moment I thought about saying something. The conversation would have gone something like: Hey, speaking of hospitals, I know you hate them and it's a whole big thing for you, but they said I should have someone with me. Depending on his reaction, I'd explain about the urine and blood tests, insist it was a simple procedure I didn't feel remotely conflicted about; it was just like going to the dentist and having a wisdom tooth out, because that's what you do with a wisdom tooth, there's no two ways about it. If he seemed uncomfortable, I'd calm him down: there'd be no reproach, no blame, no questions, I wouldn't ask anything of him except to be there, to go with me and maybe help me a bit once I was out – call a taxi, make me a cup of tea when we got home, some soup, painkillers, a blanket. That was all.

But then he asked me to come with him to see the house. He wanted me to look at the structure, see whether it would be feasible to restore, if I'd be willing to take it on. Of course I was willing. More than willing, I was thrilled we were back together again, relaxed and hatching a plan. I wasn't about to ruin it by mentioning that other thing, of course I wasn't. There'd be another chance. Or maybe it would be best to deal with it myself without ever telling him: I wouldn't want to freak him out, disturb the calm that was starting to settle over everything.

Can I have a bite? I asked him, and he pushed the pie towards me without a second thought, which confirmed that we were making progress, treading on solid ground. Usually he'd be annoyed, try to order me a slice – which I'd refuse on account of it being too much – and if he did let me try his, then he wouldn't touch it again himself.

We left the restaurant and went down Insurgentes towards Parque Hundido. We turned off at the slope leading up to the clock, unhurriedly navigating the pathways, dogs, shouting children, sweaty athletes and replicas of pre-Hispanic monuments hidden in the undergrowth. We headed over to the other side, where the hedgerows give way to a thicker wooded area. Zuri led me towards an incline and we emerged on the opposite side of the park. Across the street, behind the tulip trees, jacarandas and sweetgums, stood the house.

For a few minutes Zuri struggled with the lock on the bevelled gate, unable to find the right key. He was tense, bad-tempered – he knew the house would be dirty, infested with insects. Still, he trusted me. And that made me feel useful. Each time he tried a new key he had to clean it with a wet wipe, put away the packet, open and close the zip on his rucksack three times, and then, when the key didn't work, open and close the zip three times to get the wet wipes out again and clean the next one. He was starting to look desperate. How about we jump over? I asked. There was a ledge on the wall less than a metre off the ground, so it was easy to secure one foot, grab hold of the clay lattice and climb up. I lodged the toes of my trainers in the gaps between the fish scales, sat astride the wall and jumped down into the ditch overrun with imaginary lizards. Zuri had stayed where he was, frowning at me from the other side of the gate. It annoyed him that I did such things. He was completely unable to step over a chain between two posts, duck under the queue barrier at the bank or cross the road at a red light, even if there were no cars coming. I tried to adapt to his ways, but sometimes my common sense won out, which irritated him. Once I was on the other side of the gate, I realised the lock was bolted from the inside. It was just a question of sliding it across and then it was open.

The door to the house was made of forged ironwork and pebbled glass, framed by a thick, semi-circular cantera stone arch with baroque engravings. A classic motif of Mexico City neo-colonial mansions. You had to go up three steps to reach it. This time the lock offered no resistance. There was no warning, no omen. The gust from the open doorway stirred the dark breath nestled in the corners of the house and let the warm breeze in. Our voices shook the silence and our footprints marked the dust that had settled over the tiles.

I was eleven when I sliced off the end of my left index finger with a band saw. I'd been cutting a piece of oak for the lid of a jewellery box where I planned to keep the strawberry-shaped rose gold earrings Mum had just given me. Naturally, I was forbidden from using the machinery in the workshop, but I was alone and it seemed like the easiest thing in the world to mark the piece of wood with a pencil, press the switch and start sawing away, instead of spending who knows how many hours forcing the fret saw against the grain, only to end up with a ragged cut.

I'd used the band saw several times, albeit with my father's help. Wrapping his arms around mine, he'd guide the motion with his hands. I thought I was ready to do it by myself. I cut the sides and base. The more the teeth bit their way through the fibres along my pencil line, the more my confidence grew. It all happened very quickly. When I saw the red and the tip of my finger in the sawdust, I felt no pain, only confusion. I couldn't grasp the leap from one moment to the next, before the slicing and after it. I hid the wound in my fist, turned off the saw with my elbow and ran to my grandmother's house for my mother. She went back to the workshop for the rest of my finger, wrapped it in a piece of toilet paper and tucked it into my jumper pocket. She said they might be able to sew it back on. Thick blood streamed warmly into my sleeve. In the car, on the way to the Red Cross, a dull pain began to envelop me – not just where the wound was, but also my arm, my torso, my whole body, as though I hadn't been cut but rather beaten with a baseball bat. However, the real pain exploded later, when I was alone with the health assistants and opened my hand to show them the finger; when I took the ball of toilet paper out of my pocket and handed it to them.

The doctor examined the piece of finger under the lamplight, turned it over with a pair of tweezers, grimaced and said: It can't be saved. The exposed flesh was coated in sawdust; the wood had penetrated the tissue. No matter how carefully they washed it, the wound risked infection. He left the tissue on the tray and it finally hit me that the little scrap of flesh, complete with nail and bone, had once been part of me and was no longer. The doctor took my hand, held it under the light, touched my finger bone – and all at once the pain shot through me as though the saw were slicing into me only then, was still slicing my entire body into pieces. They injected anaesthetic into different parts of my hand and the drugs soon took effect. I felt as though I was made of foam. Nobody could hurt me. I watched, gazing dully, as the needle entered and exited my skin. I could feel the black thread pulling through each entry point. When the doctor finished sewing me up, I saw that he'd left my finger looking like a sausage, which I found terribly funny – I couldn't stop laughing. Go to sleep now, love, said the nurse on duty, but in the end my laughter was infectious and both she and the man on the next bed joined in: my finger looked like a cartoon sausage, curved

12

and swollen and knotted at the end, and it cracked me up all over again every time I saw it. At school, I had to take the bandage off several times to show the sceptics that I really had sliced off the end of my finger and the result was the funniest thing they'd ever seen. The wound scabbed over, the stitches were removed, the swelling eased and my finger lost its comic effect. At the end of my fifth year, all that was left was a pink stump I'd use to frighten my cousins and anyone who tried to make fun of me.

Curiously, far from putting me off going to the workshop, I found that the saw accident had endowed me with a special ability to use all manner of tools, to learn techniques simply by watching somebody else's hands perform them, to transform material at will. I'd paid the price – I'd been deprived of a small piece of myself and was therefore owed something in return for that propitiatory sacrifice. It was only fair.

Of course, after the incident it wasn't easy to reassure my parents, especially my mother, about my stubborn penchant for making and repairing things. She wanted to keep me close, by the sewing machine, up on the mezzanine that divided our house into the 'dust zone' and the 'dust-free zone'. Downstairs was the male domain, rough and untidy, polar opposite of the clean, domestic, female universe above. The two worlds were joined via a little ship's staircase with steps carpeted in forest green, on which we'd wipe our feet as we went up. The bottom steps were covered in sawdust, but the grime faded towards the final three, which were generally clean.

Upstairs, half of the mezzanine was occupied by rolls of fabric, a headless mannequin, a table my mother used as an ironing board and a Singer, which sat on a wooden chest with a series of long thin drawers along one side. There she kept her needles, thread and bobbins, as well as more unlikely objects – a charm shaped like the little hand of a saint, some rusted tin ornaments, a dice shaker, my great-grandfather's passport. Also on the mezzanine was the TV, an armchair draped with a crocheted blanket and the desk where I did my homework. The three of us would sit up there and eat when there wasn't time to go and see my grandmother in the other house, where all we did was sleep and shower. I spent my afternoons there between the ages of five and ten, often alone, kneeling on the carpet, absorbed in my colouring books or playing with my dolls. I'd use the rug as the floorplan for a house whose divisions were marked by encyclopaedia tomes or shoeboxes: here's the bedroom and there's the kitchen, that's the living room, over there is the garden. I'd change my doll's outfit over and over again, do her hair in plaits or a bun, such that she was never quite ready to leave for the party with her imaginary sisters, who never arrived. Very occasionally one of my cousins would play with me, although for this to happen I had to cry, beg on my knees and ask permission a thousand times. My mother's in-laws were not the most accommodating.

Back then I liked to watch my mother while she sewed. I remember the sound of her long black buttonhole scissors as she cut the fabric leisurely over the desk's hollow drum, thrrip, thrrip, thrrip, the warm round light from the hanging crystal lamp, the flake of soap she used to mark the fabric, the pins sticking out of the material or the little blue velvet ball. My mother gave me the cut-offs so I could dress my Barbies in miniature versions of the full-size pieces she made. She helped me sew them on the Singer or sat me in her lap so I could do it myself. From that cosy little nest, I'd watch my mother's mottled hands preparing the machine, oiling it, brushing away the lint, winding the thread round the right colour spool, sliding it into the grooves, careful to go through every single slot, because if you missed just one the thread would tangle under the fabric and the whole thing would be ruined. But Mum knew her Singer inside out. She did all the necessary checks and would get everything ready before finally carefully sewing the pieces together and miraculously giving body to the fabric.

Over time, however, the resinous smell of the sawdust and the roar of the machines in my father's workshop down below exerted a kind of magnetic effect on me. I'd go downstairs and scurry furtively past the hundreds of planks, logs and layers of plywood piled up against the wall, looking anxious, on tenterhooks as they awaited their turn. An almost human warmth emanated from their bodies – they had faces, eyes emerging from their cut lengths, profiles, expressions frozen mid-cry, or in a miserly smile, or a twisted grimace. I'd go to my father and watch him, intent on the act of smoothing, using a hand planer that produced perfect wooden curls.

The floor was completely carpeted in sawdust, wood shavings, strips and chips of wood of every kind. It was comforting there, out of the cold, amidst the smell of macerated forest, paint and glue. When they were sanding parota wood, though, you had to make a run for it, because the air would fill with a peppery sting that clung to your throat till you couldn't stop coughing. As soon as Dad put on his industrial facemask, my mother would pick up her handbag and purse and tell me it was time to go. We'd do the shopping more slowly than usual, lingering in the haberdasheries to look at catalogues, button samples, different shades of Gütermann thread, rolls of lace trim. We'd return once the sawdust storm had abated.

My father's willingness to surrender to the burn of the parota wood seemed to invigorate him. Wood chips served as bedding in that den of his, and he didn't like it when we swept the floor. When he went out for supplies, my mother would ask me and Señora Beatriz to help clean the workshop. On his return, my father would grumble at the naked floor and then get back to work, seeking shelter amidst the sawdust.

News had spread around the neighbourhood about my father's skill at repairing furniture, so the workshop was crammed full of wobbly tables, rocking chairs with broken bejuco seats and cupboards with their ribs exposed, shamelessly stripped of their panelling. Each piece taught me a different method, a new solution. Works in progress were set out in the clear area that divided the workshop in half: while someone sanded a set of chairs, someone else would be fixing the legs onto a table supported on two trestles, another painting a bookcase and yet another planing a table. There was always some hypnotic, methodical, repetitive action to watch, spellbound, and lose myself in.

At the back, behind the staircase, there was a school desk where Mum jotted down the woodwork orders and did the invoicing. She was the one who dealt with clients; she inspired confidence – people knew her as a seamstress and felt that the piece of furniture they'd ordered would also in some way be made to measure. My father limited himself to instructing his staff and diagnosing the furniture to be repaired. He almost always ended up saying: Yes, we can do that, of course we can, everything can be fixed. He'd even stuck on the wall next to the desk a sign that said, 'THERE'S A SOLUTION FOR EVERYTHING', then in smaller letters '(except death, an ugly face, and a broken heart)'. He'd made the same joke so many times that he got it printed and hung in a glass-less frame next to the council permits and another sign: 'We'll do the impossible right away. Miracles may take a bit longer'. Plus the 'Sánchez Carpentry' calendar, whose landscapes changed every year; come Christmas, no client would leave without one rolled up and rubber-banded under their arm.

In the shelter of those mutilated logs, I discovered the miraculous ability to shape a piece of material into something useful. Vegetation would abandon its wildness, domesticated by geometrical shapes, stylised into delicate silhouettes and perfectly smooth surfaces, into curved feet, or moulding shaped like a dove's breast. Seeing as I came down so often to watch, my father started to put me to work, handing me a piece of sandpaper or a dry paintbrush. But naturally I bored of such menial tasks. I wanted to make important things, to submit wood to the steel blade, to wind, drill, sand down, turn one thing into another. I'd get fed up, leave a plank of wood half-sanded and go back up to the mezzanine. After a while I'd head down again to try my luck a second time. It was thus that my natural stubbornness gained ground in the realm of blades and heavy machinery.

After the accident with the saw, I had to go back to square one when it came to convincing my parents, with the added aggravation that my mother was now flatly opposed. We argued and argued. She wanted me to learn crosshatch embroidery and I wanted to weave bejuco; she'd send me to dance classes, I'd go to a ceramics or wood or metal workshop, or learn how to use a potter's wheel. She'd send me to buy a metre of braided elastic and I'd escape to smoke unfiltered cigarettes: Raleighs, Gratos, Alas, Faros. To appease her, I compensated for my less refined interests with bookbinding classes, needlework, artisanal breadmaking.

As I grew, so did my restlessness. I wanted to live alone, visit all the museums, hear all the music, go to all the theatres, to cinemas where they showed European films; I wanted to understand art, pursue something more sublime than furniture and clothing, unsophisticated as they were. I don't want anything to do with your old rags, I told my mother the day she slapped me. I was almost nineteen and heading out to a café where poets drank beer and read their verses into the microphone, because one of them held a flame for me and I liked him too, though I had nothing to spend. My mother was insisting we go with my cousins to choose some fabric for the dresses we were going to wear to a wedding. Both of us lost our patience. After the slap, the weeping, the forcing open of my bedroom door with the crowbar she kept for such occasions, I confessed, still indignant, that I'd been applying to study in the capital. I was saving up for it. Neither she nor my father could dissuade me. A couple of weeks later, I said goodbye from the window of a bus that would take me away to a new life, one that was completely mine. As I left, my enormous rucksack seemed to weigh no more than a feather pillow; just enough ballast to stop my feet from rising up off the ground.

I struggled to make sense of the tone and rhythm here, to keep myself oriented according to the pre-Hispanic map of the five cardinal directions. I found a tiny apartment on the roof of an office block where I improvised a bookcase and a table, lay down first a mat and later a mattress; then came the mini fridge, the washing machine and the floral two-seater sofa that someone had abandoned in the street. Finally, I could eat in bed and leave my clothes lying on the floor, fill the place with smoke, drink on a Monday, do the ironing stark naked, read until dawn. I also changed my speech and my style, becoming pretentious, ridiculous, putting on airs and graces.

I was preparing for my first semester undergraduate exams in History of Art when I got the news: my mother was in hospital. I swallowed my pride to go to her, but there was no healing the rift between us, there wasn't time. The cystic fibrosis she had always kept at bay, almost in secret, ended up suffocating her practically overnight. After the funeral, my father wanted nothing to do with the workshop, or me, or anyone. The hospital rained debts down on him, but he didn't want any new orders. He tore down the sign he'd had printed and cursed himself for having taken death's name in vain so many times. We lost the property, the machinery, the mezzanine. He took up residence in my grandmother's house and started drinking. His hands began to tremble. His poor hands. They never learned how to be still, to do nothing.

I returned to the capital on the pretext of continuing my degree. This city is big enough to hide in, even from yourself. I went back to studying for my first semester classes and passed with an ease that propelled me smoothly into the second, third and fourth semesters. My final exam was followed by another, to get into the master's, then came the grant application, sporadic bookbinding work, the flu, conjunctivitis, books on the theory of restoration, laboratory practicals and field work, my first orders, a yellow cat called Baudelaire, the *Dictionnaire Raisonné du Mobilier Français* and Saturday courses at the Alliance Française until I could actually read it, sporadic work, jogging along leafy pavements, reading Benjamin and Bourdieu for my thesis, inventing fifty different ways to eat spaghetti, avoiding the building manager, drinking only wine, whisky and Red Bull, smoking, losing Baudelaire, walking in search of abandoned mansions, working and working and working, seeking shelter in my own kind of sawdust.

Inside, the house smelled of mouse droppings and damp. Zuri looked horrified and covered his nose with his shirt collar. I don't know if I was more amazed by the mess or by the enormous, double-height living room: I instantly pictured it transformed into a thing of beauty. Light from the big windows fell on the crumbling walls, crates and furniture, some worthless after all this time, others valuable for the same reason. There were boxes everywhere, old fashioned fixtures, obsolete devices, upholstery in discontinued fabrics, books, vintage lamps and all manner of period items that no one had bothered to cover with white sheets like they do in the films: left to ruin, laid bare to the weight of the dust.

Zuri went over to a sliding door off the front hall and tried the handle, but the runners had rusted and he could barely force it open enough for us to squeeze through. Don Eligio's library belonged to two clearly differentiated eras. First, an austere period, when the four bookcases had been fitted to the back wall and the leather-bound volumes lined up in order; when the garish diamond pattern wallpaper and thick green vinyl reading chair had been picked out; when someone decided to hang a painting of a beach with rough, blue-green waves battering the rocks, forming great white foaming masses whose movement the painter had successfully brought to life, though the piece had little else to recommend it. A severe period, like the ocean scene, which contrasted with another, vaguer, more recent time, when a mess of knick-knacks, paperbacks, old papers, receipts, boxes, folders bearing printed labels, stationery and defunct photographic artefacts had begun to populate the surfaces. This second era dominated the side of the room where the desk was, behind which was a window overlooking the street, with a Venetian blind.

I went over to inspect the double portrait on the wall by the window: the same childlike face trapped within two ovals of gold-rimmed card. The one on the left was higher than the one on the right, and this calculated irregularity created a sense of harmony, less disconcerting than if the ovals had been lined up like two eyes. That's Silvia and María, Zuri said without coming over to look. I remembered him mentioning Silvia, the aunt whose house smelled of sour milk, and before I could ask about María he explained that they were twins. He'd heard about María when he was little; she was an actress who'd appeared in several Hollywood films. When he saw photos of her as a child, he thought such a beautiful woman couldn't possibly be related to him. Unfortunately, she died tragically and very young: she slit her own throat with a shaving knife. Zuri remembers finding the newspaper cutting between the pages of an album and said that he'd still been struck by her beauty, even though the photo showed her lying face down in a pool of blood. I reassessed the portrait in the light of this tale. Both girls had very black hair and expressive eyes. One of them was smiling, the other serious. I thought the melancholy-looking one must be

María and that this trait must have been at the root of her misfortune.

Zuri was examining the spines of the books. I asked him what he was looking for, but he was so engrossed he didn't respond. I went and sat in the chair behind the desk and began to nose about. There's something about old stationery that fascinates and repulses me in equal measure. Maybe it's the futility of it, or perhaps it's the peculiar way grime collects in the corners, the faint smell of the greasy hands it belonged to. Clips end up swimming in dust, the springs in staplers and hole-punches start to squeak, old spillages crack, liquids solidify, paper yellows and the wood and graphite of pencils harden; envelope glue sweetens and Sellotape melts like bitter caramel. Amidst the scribbled diaries and calendars stamped with the year 1992 or 1987, business cards, empty cheque books, faded purchase receipts and faxes, there were several books lying open, face down in a pile. I picked up the first: stories by Perrault, an illustration depicting the moment the woman opens the door to the forbidden room. The caption read: She went so quickly down the dark little stairway that she almost cracked her head open. The second was a red book with a Chinese character printed on the cover. The third was in French; it looked like an old surgical manual. Its pages showed neat, clear prints of a hand chopping off a limb; a cut made with a precision instrument, no fluid, no pain. The cutting hand exerted no force, the limbs offered no resistance, the muscles not even contracting. I read aloud a phrase at random, in an exaggerated accent: *Une coupe transversale divise alors les téguments internes un peu au dessous du lieu de la ponction...* Zuri turned, came over and snatched it away with an urgency verging on violent. He also took the book with the red cover and put both away in his rucksack. I asked if I could keep the Perrault.

Zuri had been devoted to photography ever since he was twelve. Nothing else mattered to him. He hurled himself into it with a care and passion I've never seen in anyone else. Photography was his life in the most literal sense. He told me once that he had always suffered from epilepsy and neuropsychiatric complications that prevented him from going to a normal school. He'd studied with private teachers, had few friends, couldn't watch TV or play videogames. The internet bored him, but his fragile health meant he wasn't allowed to use it anyway.

Early one morning, when he heard the electric mechanism of the front gate, he went out into the garden to see it opening for an emerald-green Impala convertible he didn't recognise. Through the window, the driver asked if his grandfather was home. He wasn't, Zuri replied. The man asked if his mum was there, and again Zuri said no. The man thought for a few seconds and then said: Do you want to come with me? I'm your uncle Eligio, your grandfather's cousin. I'm going to a hacienda in Morelos to take some photos, we'll be back tonight. Zuri, angry at having been left alone again, was starting to show the first signs of prepubescent rebellion, so he gave a lopsided shrug, walked round the front of the Impala and got into the passenger seat.

He spent the whole morning lugging cameras and tripods around, bored and hungry. He couldn't see why his great uncle spent so much time on a single shot, adjusting the variables hundreds of times before pressing the shutter. Back then, Zuri thought all you had to do was put your eye to the viewfinder and shoot. He was fed up of standing in the sun with a relative he didn't know, arms crossed listlessly, fed up with his uncle's maddening, trivial orders: pass me a new cartridge, no, not that one, the 35mm, the green one. Take that bag to the car. Bring me the bag you put away. Hold the screen here. Steady, hold your arms up, higher, a bit to the right. Not so far, a bit to the left. The payoff came when that same day his great uncle placed his old Nikon FM2 in Zuri's hands for the first time. Zuri peered through the rectangle and was surprised to discover that this new eye allowed him to portion out his world at will. He aimed the viewfinder at the sun and took a picture. Not like that, Don Eligio said, and showed him how to control the light and depth of field, how to breathe and frame and gauge exactly when to take the shot. 'Your vision has to be scalpel-sharp'. He pointed to his right eye, pulling down the lower lid. 'You have to learn to cut with your eyes before cutting with the camera.'

Zuri was fascinated. He didn't want to put the Nikon down. He kept taking photos the whole way home, even though the roll of film had long since finished. As he went into the house, Don Eligio said: Keep it. You can come to the lab at weekends, if you like, and I'll teach you to develop. Half the work's in the shot, the other half's in the darkroom.

Naturally, his mum was horrified, saying she'd never allow that heartless bastard anywhere near her son again.

Turned out, the invitation to Morelos had been no innocent outing, but rather an opportunity to provoke his grandfather, with whom Don Eligio had had an irreparable falling out. In any case, no number of tears from his mother nor reprimands from his grandfather could dampen Zuri's enthusiasm for photography. He'd found the perfect way to perceive the world and nobody could take that away from him.

Flakes of dry green paint crunched underfoot as we went up the stairs. The tips of an ivy plant had snuck in through the broken skylight, threatening to rewild the place. We reached the second floor. There were six doors off the landing: three on the right, three on the left. In the middle, opposite the staircase, a balcony with a Roman balustrade overlooked the double-height living room below: the sofas, the tall windows, the fireplace. We passed shapeless bundles, boxes and upended furniture; Zuri was struggling to ignore the dirt, the dust, the mouse droppings and the stink of mould and ammonia. He went straight to the only door that was ajar, the third on the left.

We entered a large, dirty, gloomy bedroom. A furniture set bearing Chinese motifs was barely visible beneath the mess and the dust. Seen from inside, the balconies seemed less sumptuous, lacking in mystery; they were obscured by ordinary curtains printed with orange pagodas and willow trees against a grimy background. There was a smell of rancid grease, something ancient and male. At the back of the room, French doors gave onto a little terrace. We stepped out. The balcony looked over a side street. In one corner, a large, parched flowerpot cradled the skeletons of aloe veras and mallows. On the other side, a staircase led straight up to the attic.

We paused for a moment on the terrace, as though Zuri had already known what we would find and wanted to inflate his own sense of anticipation. He leaned over the balustrade and set about rolling a cigarette. I peered down into the street. I could have said something about the house, its style, the restoration. I wanted to ask if he was OK, because clearly he was not, but I decided to keep quiet. The place demanded silence. I gestured for a drag of his cigarette, but when I passed it back he held up a hand to say he didn't want it anymore. I stubbed it out in the dirt and followed him.

From the street, I'd imagined the attic to be a narrow tower, but it was really quite spacious. The arched windows framed the light: three in the wall on the left and another three looking out to the street beside the park. From below they'd seemed as slender as filigree, so I was disconcerted by their true scale, as though with the change in perspective the house had grown big enough to devour us.

The space was surprisingly uncluttered, though the piles against the wall opposite the arches looked like theatrical stage machinery: cardboard columns, wall hangings, imperial style armchairs, drapes with dull, brass-coloured tassels, sad plastic palm trees and limp cloth flowers that must have served as the backdrops to Don Eligio's portraits. A pile of boxes under a tarp caught Zuri's attention. He lifted a corner, wary at first, then gave the tarp a firm tug in spite of the dust. Below, he was amazed to discover his great uncle's collection of old cameras, intact, perfectly packed and ready to use. He set about moving the boxes from one side to another, reading the labels, explaining the virtues of each item in a murmur. He took the lids off the cases and boxes and examined each artefact, spellbound, like a child waking up on Christmas morning and opening all his presents by himself.

While Zuri inspected the boxes I went over to the arched windows and watched people walking around the perimeter of the park. Beside the console table there was a trunk and an ottoman. The trunk wasn't locked, so I assumed it was alright for me to nose around. I crouched down and was hit with the reek of mothballs mixed with paper and ink and emulsion. I carefully removed packets of brown paper, boxes of negatives, notebooks, books, letters and thick stacks of photos of Don Manuel Álvarez Bravo, Lola, Nacho López, most of them bearing dedications; I sat down on the floor and shuffled through a few. They were incredible. There were several copies of the famous photograph of a wasp-waisted woman in a fifties-style dress walking down a Mexico City street as the men around her eat her up with their eyes. There was Frida Kahlo with her Xoloitzcuintle dogs, several prints of Casasola's classic Adelita, and costumbrista scenes of women in shawls on cobbled streets, rural labourers in sombreros, coarse cloth trousers and huaraches, women from Tehuantepec in flowery huipil blouses, white houses with tiled roofs.

Zuri came over and opened one of the boxes of negatives, holding them up to the light. I didn't feel I had the right to flick through the notebooks and open the letters covered in airmail stickers and stamps from all over the world, but he did. Entranced, hands trembling, he shared some of his discoveries with me. I'd never seen him so happy. Among the letters, we found the cruel, macabre photograph of the *leng tch'e* torture method, death by a thousand cuts: a square packed with onlookers and three men holding the prisoner's bonds as the executioner amputates his left leg. Laid open like a star, the bones of his thorax exposed, the prisoner smiles serenely; his eyes look skyward, lit up in quiet surrender to the relief of death. It was an old photo, black and white. The dark blood seeped into the shadows. I didn't want to give it much importance. The image felt so remote that it had lost the value of reality and was now merely an object: dark stains on a rectangular piece of card. I remember turning the print over and reading the words written on the back: 'Is there anything more tenacious than memory? – Chava, August 1962.' The unruly handwriting in sepia ink had paled to amber and the corners of the paper had darkened more than the middle, as though time had sensed the weight of the words written there and had wanted to illuminate them.

We first met in the library at the Mora Institute. I was reading for my final exams when I heard the double click of a shutter. I looked up and saw the eye of the camera, focused not on me but on the stub of my left index finger: on my hand in my hair, its truncated finger twisting a single lock. At first I felt embarrassed, exposed. Reflexively, I hid behind the covers of my Jackson and Day manual. I straightened my back and tucked my hair behind my ear, though by then he'd turned around and was heading towards the exit.

Once I'd recovered from the surprise, curiosity kicked in. A stranger had seen me exactly as I had wanted to be seen, had aimed the viewfinder at the very spot and taken a moment for himself, a moment that no longer belonged to my body, a fragment of me, like the fingertip I'd kept in formaldehyde for years; the skin had yellowed, wrinkling darkly, and the nail turned an iridescent gold. We were told formaldehyde was toxic, so we had to take the jar to a hospital. They poured the liquid into a black container and put the flesh in a yellow bag stamped with the symbol for dangerous-infectious-biological waste. I asked what they would do with it, and the technician told me it would be incinerated. Everything was incinerated: bits of skin, gall bladders, bandages. A piece of me dissolved along with other people's ashes, while I went on living. Now, suddenly, a man had appeared with his camera and unveiled the secret of the propitiatory sacrifice; he had taken a photo of its emblem, and I needed to see it.

I went after him, leaving my things where they were: my pearled jumper hanging on the back of the chair, the block of notes on the table with my books, my Bic pen, my rucksack in the locker. I spotted the back of his green bomber jacket between the trimmed hedges, right by the exit. I'd have to run. By the time I finally reached the gate, he was about to turn the corner. I wanted to shout out something to stop him, but I didn't know what. Hey you, hey man, hey mate. None seemed right, so I said very loudly: Photographer! A long, strange word I heard escape from my mouth with deep 'o's and whistling 'f's. He turned around at once. I walked a few paces and once I was close enough, I asked: Can I see the photo? His eyebrows furrowed in confusion.

'The one you just took of me in there,' I said, and held up my left hand to show him my 4.6 fingers. 'I'd really like to see it.'

'It's analogue', he said, instead of replying that it wasn't possible.

'Sorry?'

'It's a film camera.' He took the machine out of his rucksack and showed me the black hatch covered in fake leather where the screen should have been.

Then it was my turn to frown and pout. I must have looked like a child who'd dropped her ice cream. I suppose this softened him.

He glanced at his watch. 'I can give you a print, if you like.'

'Yes! Please… I mean, assuming it doesn't cost a fortune.'

'I'd only need the cost of the materials. I'm going to develop these rolls later. If you'll be in the library tomorrow, I can drop it off.'

'Wait, you develop them yourself?'

'Uh huh.'

'Seriously? With trays and an old bathtub and washing lines, like in the films?'

'Ah… not quite.'

'Sorry, it's just I've never met anyone who still works with those kinds of photos.'

'Well, it's quite common. More than it should be.' He wore a look of faint disdain. I liked it.

'I've never seen the process. It must be kind of magical.'

'I mean, it's just chemistry, but yeah, a kind of magic, I guess.' He looked towards a side street.

'Is it far, where you develop the photos?'

'No, it's just here, a couple of blocks.'

'Can I come with you? I promise to stay in a corner and not get in the way.'

I saw his face and knew I'd gone too far, as usual: that kind of thing isn't on, girl, it's rude, leave people alone, don't be a nuisance, don't touch anything, don't get too close. I smiled. What was I to do?

'I guess…' He gave a lopsided shrug and started walking.

I followed him down the narrow pavements of Colonia San Juan Mixcoac, wet with recent rain. The studio was on Calle Poussin, behind the library. A collective had set up in what had been an old vecindad: a long courtyard with a cement floor and five or six little single storey flats, which must have been squalid before the outdoor sinks, junk, clothes lines and gas tanks were cleared and the walls painted white, the ironwork black and pots of cactuses and succulents arranged around the place. The photography studio was in the biggest room, an L-shaped one right at the back. To get in, you had to go through the strangest door: it had an ingenious mechanism, an inner cylinder that revolved until its opening coincided with that of an outer one. Entering the space, you had to turn the mechanism until the opening was on the inside, allowing you to enter and exit without any light getting in. I thought it looked like part of some intergalactic spaceship. Zuri went in first to show me how the door worked and to turn on the light. Inside, the room was painted black from floor to ceiling; the windows were bricked up to keep out even the slightest crack of light. There was a sink with three taps and four heavy-duty water bottles lined up next to it, racks of materials on the walls and a long high table by the entrance. This is the developing area, Zuri said. As you can see, no bath, no clothes lines.

The bedroom next door was the printing area, separated off by a heavy black curtain that Zuri drew aside to show me the enlargers, drawing table, drying rack and trays, each with its own pair of tongs. He let the curtain fall and we went back to the wet room. Zuri took three rolls of film from the pocket of his bomber jacket and put them on the countertop along with the camera, a little black developing tank, some scissors and three developing cartridges. He warned me he'd have to turn off the light. I pressed my back against the wall and stood motionless under the cool weight of the dark. The back of my optic nerve cast waves of colour that spilled onto the black background before slowly fading away. I could feel the fibres of my oculomotor nerve relaxing; my irises were fully dilated, finally finding the relief they'd craved ever since the invention of electric light:

complete, unbounded darkness, eyes wide open, adrift in an absolute sea.

As my eyes got used to the pitch black, other senses rallied: the earthy, mineral smell of the solutions used for developing; a provocative smell, not unlike the chlorine that lingers between your fingers after swimming in a pool, a smell our infatuated noses seek out and kiss. Beneath the chemicals, I could just about catch the scent of his breath, heavy and alive. I listened to his breathing, his far-off heartbeat, his heat. I could hear his hands scratch at the silence with precise, ritualistic movements. The fragile crunch of the cartridges as they broke open were like nuts in the most delicate of shells, the sigh of the film as it unwound in his fingers, the click of the cartridge, the hiss of the polymer unspooling in obedient spirals. New sounds, new smells, a body nearby in the dark, borderless, sightless, faceless. Just energy, exhalation, voice; proximity, not too far, but not close enough to touch. The two of us, dissolved in the shadows.

Suddenly, the peace was broken by the unmistakable sound of a chain: metal on metal. I heard Zuri run to the entrance, shout Don Jacinto! and try to move the cylinder, but he couldn't. The chain was obstructing the revolving mechanism.

'Did you leave it open?' he asked me accusingly, alarmed.

Baffled, I didn't reply. Leave what open?

'Did you turn it back? Did you leave the opening on the outside?'

'I don't know!' I said, distressed. 'I think so?'

Zuri shook the mechanism, smacked his palm against the metal and shouted again for Jacinto, beating and kicking harder and harder in desperation. My dilated pupils could barely decipher shadows, agitated movement, tension. Zuri put the rolls of film in the tank and tightened the lid. He flicked the light switch three four times, but nothing happened. He hammered on the door again and shouted, but it was useless. Don Jacinto, seeing the light off and the door cylinder open, had assumed there was no one inside and padlocked the door, as he did every afternoon before leaving. He switched everything off at the mains, took his straw-coloured jacket down off the hook and left two hours early, because the game had already started; he'd been listening on his headphones but wanted to watch the end at home.

Though I couldn't see his face in the darkness, it was clear Zuri's reaction was way out of proportion to what was happening: his panting intensified into short, rapid breaths, then yielded to a silence that alarmed me and made me reach out a cautious hand until I found him crouched in a corner. I felt the cold skin of his cheeks, the streaming sweat, his stiff shoulders. I crouched down and began to wrap my arms around him from behind. It's OK, I murmured, deep breaths. His head was tucked into his chest. I hugged his torso and felt his racing heart under my hand. They say a panic attack is as stressful and painful as a heart attack, that it's like having an explosive device strapped to the middle of your chest, that death throbs imminent with every heartbeat and even though you're breathing there isn't enough air to stop you from suffocating. I didn't know what to do, all I could think was to cradle him in my arms, rest my head against his and say the same things I would have said to a frightened child. The muscles of his chest gradually relaxed and his skin began to warm up. We stayed like that for a long time, lulling the silence, until he became a dead weight between my knees. I clenched my jaw in tender longing.

Some time later, Zuri told me about when his condition had first made itself known. He was four or five years old. The sight of Faquir, calm and proud as a sphinx, his snout stained with blood, prey clutched between his paws, had etched itself into his memory in vivid detail; there was another small creature at the foot of the tree, one in the reeds at the edge of the pond, a fourth coming apart in the water. A carpet of red and white feathers, red and white like candy canes. He remembered the Weimaraner's shining, satisfied air. Zuri stood there, enjoying the scene, which was lit by the first rays of sun. He wanted to be Faquir's accomplice, to keep his secret, now that he knew about secrets. But how could he keep a secret so red and wild? He let his friend go on enjoying the warmth of the bird flesh between his lips and returned to the empty, silent house. The only person at home was his grandfather, who was still asleep; he always took out his hearing aids before bed, so he hadn't noticed a thing. His mother had been out for the night; his father had left a couple of weeks earlier and there was no one to throw the ball to Faquir, so he'd go and fetch it from among the reeds and disturb the peace of the orange carp who ploughed the muddy bottom. Zuri went back to his room and got into bed. He fell into a deep sleep and woke when the sun was high in the sky to the sound of Faquir barking in the distance, locked in his cage, clawing away like a mad thing. He heard the rough murmur of the sprinklers watering the garden, his grandfather's footsteps in the corridor. He stayed very still under the blanket, trying to ignore the need to pee. He heard the lock turn in his bedroom door, the footsteps retreating, the sprinklers, the furious barking, the crunch of the metal hammer, the shot, the squeal, the sprinklers, the silence. By the time his mother woke him, he had wet the bed, his face was completely blue, his pulse barely discernible.

The attack began to recede. I breathed in the smell of his hair, his warmth. The heavy abandon of his body pressing into mine sent such a rush of tenderness through me I could barely stop myself from smothering him in my arms. A few minutes later Zuri got up, himself once again, to face the facts of an absurd reality: we were locked in. My pupils had dilated enough to see his silhouette as he felt about, searching for something to break the lock with. The obvious thing would have been to call someone to come and let us out, but Zuri didn't use a mobile phone – doctor's orders – or any kind of device that emitted alerts and notifications. He had an ancient phone he kept switched off at home, turning it on only occasionally. Mine was in the locker at the Institute, which had probably closed by now. It must be eight or nine pm. I was cold and didn't want to think about the possibility of needing the toilet, because my only option would have been the sink.

We tried using a broom handle as a lever, but the handle broke. We tried slicing the fibreglass cylinder with a box cutter, but the scratches never made it to the other side. In the printing area there was a window with black painted glass, but it had been soldered into place. There was nothing to do except wait for Don Jacinto to come back in the morning. That, and stoically repress the first deep throb of my bladder.

We sat in silence on the counter, feet dangling. The rolls of film can't stay there, he said suddenly. He jumped down in the dark, picked up the tank, filled it with water and tipped it out. One by one he groped for the different bottles: the developer, the fixer, the stop bath. Without the help of a timer, he counted the seconds and swills of the tank in one direction and then the other, turn it twice, three times, tip it out, let the water run, fill it up, count the seconds and the swills, turn twice, turn three times, rinse again, let the water run, repeat the process in a sequence as exact as the notes of a concert. He would make no mistake, he could perform it with his eyes closed, this ceremony that liberated the light entrapped in every image.

Zuri set about drying the developed prints, then sat down beside me on the counter again. He was almost like a magician, finishing his act with dignified exhaustion, still porous and vulnerable to a kind of trance. He leant on my shoulder and I put my arm round him. We lay down right there. I wrapped myself round him from behind, sheltering him in the curve of my body until we fell asleep. We awoke to the light and the sound of the door. Another member of the collective had arrived early to pick up something or other. I didn't stop to learn more, just dashed out in search of the bathroom. By the time I got back, fresh faced and relieved, Zuri had gone.

I bumped into him several days later in the Village Café by Parque Hundido. I'd just got back from a run and was hugely embarrassed by how sweaty and dishevelled I was, and that I hadn't brushed my teeth. He was impeccable, as always, his style simple and austere: always jeans, Converse, a printed T-shirt under his bomber jacket, a grey woollen jumper if it was cold. His hands smelled of plain soap. Only when we drew close for a hug could I smell the soft halo of Chanel Allure mixed with the clean scent of his body. Whenever I was reminded of his smell while doing something else, I felt a damp prickle between my legs and my face flushed. I ran into him again a couple of times in that same café, dressed properly now. I'd abandoned exercise in favour of pretending to read at one of the tables, hoping he'd walk in. I liked imagining him hidden among the trees in the park, watching me through a long-range lens. I'd comb my fingers through my hair, straighten my neck, suck in my belly, strike the most ridiculous poses.

By the time we bumped into each other in the hallway of San Juan Church, my intentions were fairly obvious. He was photographing a wedding when I spotted him in the distance and crossed the street to say hello. I hesitated as I approached, not wanting to interrupt, but he smiled, turned to glance at the relatives who were about to leave, and walked over to me. We gave each other a dry kiss on the cheek. I have something of yours, he said, referring to the photo, and I suggested we meet up for a drink when he was finished. I sketched a three-line map and gave it to him. Number 9 Calle Valencia, flat 804.

'What's your drink? Beer, wine, whisky…'

'What whisky have you got?'

'Black Label…'

'How about I bring a Talisker?'

In truth, this sounded like an unthinkable luxury. I'd never tried it, only read that it was very good. Whisky was my favourite drink, even though my budget didn't stretch to decent malts. In fact, I'd been bluffing when I'd said Black Label; it would have meant no small sacrifice to fill that hole in my accounting, though I'd have made it gladly.

By the time the doorbell rang it was 11.30pm and I was putting away the sticks of jícama, cream cheese, pâté, palm hearts and olives I'd laid out for us to nibble on. I'd of course made sure I had clean sheets and was wearing nice underwear. That night, though, the surprising thing wasn't the sex, which is never particularly successful on first attempts, nor the deep, woody taste of the Talisker; what took my breath away, and my peace of mind, were the contact sheets he'd brought. There he was, in his entirety: on a dozen sheets of thick, letter-sized paper, he laid himself bare. He'd also blown up a print of my photo, as promised: I appeared in profile, the stub of my finger tucked into my hair, my eyes on the book. The image was completely unlike how I had imagined it. I looked different. The photo didn't flatter me or make me look pretty; in fact, it was disturbing. Seeing myself drawn by the light in that instant, trapped in that precise convergence of lines, made me feel strangely like I no longer belonged to myself, but to him. A body's sweet surrender to the gaze. In his photo, from his perspective, I had become someone else, someone more real. I don't know how his prints managed to capture a different dimension of reality to the one he'd photographed, a deeper, broader meaning; for example, an ear of wheat broken into the shape of a seven, or a bird's wing barely eluding a cat's jaws. Even the photos of material textures, like a knot in a tree, logs turned to ash or the collapsed ridge of a sand dune, produced the discomfort of damage to people more than to things. The National and Tame Impala played on my computer as I examined the contact sheets through a magnifying glass. I could read him there, just as he'd read me when he took that photograph. We didn't need to say anything at all.

Zuri tucked the terrible photo between the pages of a book, closed the trunk and put his arms around me tenderly, pleased, as if I'd offered him the camera collection as a gift. As if I myself were the gift. He translated his longing onto my body. We shared a long, hungry kiss, the first in ages, and lay down on the ottoman. He wanted to keep going, but I gently extracted myself and sat up on the edge. Look – that must be it over there, I said.

At breakfast, Zuri had asked what I knew about porcelain, because Don Eligio had charged him with cleaning a Chinese vase that was somewhere in the house. The family would need it for the ceremony. I said I didn't know much, but I could put him in touch with an expert. I went over for a closer look. It wasn't really a vase, to be precise, but a blue and white porcelain vessel covered in filigree, with two large characters painted on either side of its belly. The marble-coloured background, the cracks in the vitrification and the notches on the edge of the lid were proof of its authenticity. Let's go, Zuri said, hooking his rucksack over his shoulder. I picked up the vase to look at the artisan's seal on the bottom, and as I held it I felt a strange weight in my hands, a shifting that piqued my curiosity. Without thinking, I lifted the lid. I was caught off guard by a vile stench that clutched my throat as if with claws. Zuri turned to see what was going on. I hadn't caught my breath enough to explain, just gestured for him to back off: the back of my hand pressed to my nose, eyes watering, a shake of my head. Ignoring me, he came closer and peered in.

First he froze, completely paralysed, his face twisted into a grimace of repulsion, his forehead pearled with sweat. I set the vase on the ground and replaced the lid. Panic-stricken, Zuri went down to the terrace, leaned against the big clay flowerpot and retched, panting and coughing. I went over and placed a hand on his back in an attempt to comfort him, but he shook me off violently and returned inside, lurched down the stairs and slammed the door behind him. I leaned over the edge and saw him running out onto the street toward the park, where he vanished among the paths. I returned to the attic.

I spotted a roll of plastic bags amidst the mess and pulled two of them over my hands like gloves. I removed the lid again, carefully this time. The inside was coated in a dry, dark layer of something seemingly organic. It reeked, but I didn't find it quite so unbearable anymore. It wouldn't be hard to clean. There was a tap under the stairs. I opened it and a great bubbling jet of rusty water exploded onto the tiles. I was about to turn it off when a smooth, clear stream spouted forth and cleared the dust on its way down the drain. I cupped my hands and received the water like a blessing. It was as cool and limpid as from a mountain spring and looked good enough to drink. I rinsed the inside of the vase several times and watered the dead roots of the aloe and mallow plants. Then I scrubbed my hands and splashed my face. I wrapped the blue and white porcelain in the bedspread from the room with the Chinese furniture, placed the parcel inside multiple plastic bags and knotted each bag tightly enough to keep the stench in.

My knees trembled as I made my way down the stairs. I looked for Zuri as I crossed the park, but I didn't see him at the little cement tables or any of our benches or in the patch of grass where we often lay in the sun. I walked the paths, glancing all around. Fortunately, the vase wasn't too heavy, but dogs stopped to sniff the bag and I sensed that passers-by could catch the stink. I walked faster. I reached my apartment with the vague hope that Zuri would be waiting at the front door, but he wasn't. I supposed that he'd need to feel safe again, as he always did during one of his crises; to seek shelter in his asepsis, strip down, burn his clothes, open and close every door seven times, switch every light on and off seven times, submerge himself seven times in the Jordan River.

I found the car keys in my bag, so I didn't even need to go inside. I went to the corner where I'd parked, opened the boot, laid the vase inside and set out for the Zona Rosa. On Saturdays the passageways of the Plaza del Ángel were teeming with vendors. It was around three in the afternoon and many of the stalls were packing up. I wove my haphazard way among the tarps spread on the ground, following my nose, overcome with the scavenging pleasure of a shell-hunter on the beach. I reached the stall belonging to Marce, the only friend I'd made at university. I found her sitting in a lawn chair next to her wares. She greeted me matter-of-factly, as if we saw each other all the time. That was always how it felt between us: we respected each other's reticence. We understood each other that way. I showed her the package I was carrying, explained what it was and asked her to give it a look. We went into her stall. Hundreds of porcelain pieces balancing delicately on shelves and long, skinny-legged stands. I tucked my elbows into my sides, terrified of breaking something, while Marce confidently manoeuvred her hefty frame like a bear taking a stroll through the oaks. Behind the display case was a shelf crammed with a mess of materials and tools, or perhaps merely organised according to the rules of everyday use. Marce turned on a swing-arm magnifying lamp, donned her bifocals and peeled open the bags, professional as a doctor examining a patient, unperturbed by their foetid secretions. She studied the piece meticulously. Then she set it upside-down and showed me the late-nine-teenth-century Qing dynasty seal.

'What do you think? Is it worth restoring?' I asked.

'Well, Kraak ware is pretty commonplace.' Her voice was thick, a little brusque. 'Pieces like these are usually worth more for what they represent than what they cost.'

'What does this bit mean?' I pointed to one of the symbols painted on the belly.

'That's *tiān*, the ideogram for creative power and for the sky. I think this other one is *kuài*, something that breaks or has finally broken. Given the smell and the type of residue, I'd say it was used as a canopic vase, for storing organs removed during mummification. It sounds macabre, but I've seen worse, believe me. Do you want to leave it here?'

'I'm not sure. I was thinking of restoring it myself. Do you think it'll be difficult?'

'Nah, it's easy. You'll have to wash it first with Zote soap and a fibreless sponge. Then soak it overnight in a ten per cent ammonia solution, rinse it with white vinegar, let it dry and apply a stain-removal paste. You can use one I've got here if you want, it's meant for this kind of porcelain. Then eventually remove the paste with a flannel. I don't see any cracks, but if you find some, just bring it back and we'll seal them.'

She puffed a bit as she spoke. Her curt manner sparked a strange fondness in me, one I exercised by staying at arm's length. I smiled. I felt like I was back in a world I'd left a long time ago and hadn't realised I'd missed. I wished I could stay with her all afternoon, sit in silence in her lawn chair, enjoying her honest presence and her rudeness toward nosy would-be customers who never bought anything.

The label on the tube of peroxide paste reminded me that the cost of materials was one of the reasons I'd been forced to stop restoring. That said, I knew it wasn't even an eighth of what Marce would have charged a customer to clean the vase, so I paid and thanked her for sharing the steps with me. Her generosity was no small matter, considering how jealously many restorers guard their formulae.

I was pleased. I'd reconnected with my delight in repairing what was broken, recovering old things from abandonment, burnishing time. On my way back, I stopped for supplies. I didn't have a yard, so I filled the bathtub with the solution and submerged the porcelain vase. The smell of ammonia was so strong it made my eyes water. Though I preferred its piercing chemical tang over the lethal stench of the residue I'd cleaned, which kept flashing into my consciousness like a ghost.

I watch you come and go, back and forth across the attic, absorbed in the details, scrupulous, surly. I watch how tactfully you arrange each instrument on the tabletop: the ultraviolet filter, the neutral density filter, the multicoloured filters to achieve specific effects, even though it's a black and white film. I take a sip of whisky and lie back on the ottoman. Satisfied, I regard the rafters, now free of dust and cobwebs. The wax smell mixes with the scent of fresh paint on the walls. The newly polished parquet gleams as if spread with honey. I focus on you again. I watch you, but nothing can shake your concentration, you don't even look up. You're placing the cameras on the shoe plate of each tripod. The lenses, the accessories tucked away in cases with compartments specially designed for each object, they're all resting now on the black cloth you have laid out on the side table. Your face stern, your gestures solemn, you assign each item its particular place. You look worried, as if getting the details precisely right were a matter of life and death.

'You, sir, are meticulous in the extreme,' I tease, raising my voice theatrically, 'a characteristic that has

51

undoubtedly contributed to making you the most skilful photographer in the world.'

You glance up, raise an eyebrow, and smile, but quickly return to your business. Every time I see you work, I find myself jarred by your surrender, surprised by the care you devote to every action, every movement. I admire this diligence, although your co-workers at the agency criticise you for taking everything so seriously; some say outright that you're a snob, others just avoid you, especially the models, who complain that you treat them like chairs or boxes of cereal.

Take off your clothes, please. Your tone is cold and I pause, startled, as if I hadn't heard properly. You crouch in a corner to open an old green suitcase. Take off your clothes, Min, you repeat impatiently, rummaging inside the open valves. You stand, step closer, and hand me a white muslin dress without so much as a glance. Right. Now I'm the cereal box: another object you have to control if the photo series is to come out perfectly.

I decide to play along. I go to the back of the attic and shelter behind a lacquered folding screen painted with scenes from the Far East, as if I were actually embarrassed to strip in front of you. I hold the dress up in my hands: languid, lightweight, many-layered, with a sweetheart neckline and a large translucent piece covering the back, shoulders, torso and arms, like a dragonfly's sleek wings. If it weren't cocktail-length, it would look like a bridal dress. I wonder who it belonged to. It seems old. I feel the anticipatory pang of sheathing my body in someone else's garments. I give it a little shake and another look before I slip it on. In any case, it's only a prop, only a scene. I take off my jeans, t-shirt, hoodie. I take the dress and search its millefeuille for the inside lining, insert my head and swim through the fabric until I find the exit on the other side. Then the layers settle over my body. It's a little tight around the waist and I have to hold my breath for the zipper to make it up my right side. Once it's on, I let my body adjust to the cloth's embrace. I lift my arms to feel the touch of the mantilla from neck to hands, flap my wings as if longing to fly, and seek your eye to see if you've joined the game, but you're still engrossed in your labours.

You ask me to pull my hair up, leaving a few locks loose to catch the light. I lift my mane and stand in front of the mirror. I'm delighted to find myself confronted with someone new, antiquated, beautiful, cruel. I watch you in the reflection behind me. The light from the oil lamp is dim and warm. The flame dazzles me and I can barely make out your shape in the darkness; for an instant you look taller, larger than usual. I do a double-take over my shoulder, but the effect vanishes as you step closer to the light. You make sure the cameras are arranged at their respective angles according to the frame: the 4x5 Graflex Speed Graphic, the Kodak 2 Porthole, the Rolleiflex reflex, the Hasselblad hanging from your neck. You adjust intensities and distances. The plates, the medium-format rolls, the Ilford Pan 400, the 35mm Fp4 all wait on the black cloth. All symmetrically aligned in the order you'll be using them.

I sit at the griffin-foot console table and review the instructions: I need to keep my back straight, my shoulders relaxed, my torso at forty-five degrees, my head inclined slightly forwards. I must pick up the three Chinese coins on the tabletop and shake them between my hands, not too much or too little, three or four times, enough for chance to do its work, set it free, give it room to decide: let its eye open in the dark and reveal the sign. I have to toss the coins onto the marble surface, allow them to flip from side to side, to dance in circular oscilla- tions over the cold, polished stone until they fall still, and until their stillness opts for one of two sides: yin or yang, straight line or wavy. Then, right away, I need to make a horizontal mark on a sheet of paper with black charcoal: broken line or unbroken, depending. I must repeat this six times, drawing the corresponding line above the previous one each time, as if performing a brief scene of silent theatre. Six acts, a single instant when the other superimposed instants are revealed.

I take the three Chinese coins and hear the camera click. I look in the mirror and convince myself I'm not me, I'm someone else, a nameless woman who wants to read her fortune, even though she already knows it. I nestle the coins in my cupped hands. I hear the second click and the third. I shake them. You're very tense, Min, relax your shoulders, you scold me from the shadows. I take a deep breath and suppress a tickle of fear. I drop the coins onto the surface. I hear the metal clinking on the polished stone, the sharp oscillations deciphering the sign as the clicks continue one by one, far more plodding and spaced out than usual. The light is faint and the camera shutters must be opening and closing very slowly: a dragging sound, then a pause, then a second dragging sound, not unlike the footfall of someone making their way up the stairs.

The coins fall still. Three yins make a yin. I draw a broken line on the page, a line interrupted by a short blank space. First line: restore what was damaged by the father.

Ever since the night we drank Talisker and he showed me his contact sheets, we'd been going out more often, although we never discussed the terms of our relationship. I was taking the last seminars of my master's then, one on the theory of architectural intervention and another on Viollet-le-Duc. I had a job in the architecture department, filling out forms as part of my work-study requirement for the scholarship I had, and was supposed to be handing in the third chapter of my thesis, for which I'd requested three extensions and was on the verge of needing a fourth. Zuri was getting exploited from Monday to Friday at an advertising agency, so we could only see each other on Saturdays. We'd have breakfast at Marie Callender's, same booth, same order; then we'd drive my car to some historical site, visit museums, boulevards, parks, or head out of the city for Cuernavaca, Malinalco, Tepotzlán, Mineral del Chico. He'd take photos; I'd just watch. I liked to imagine the way he discovered reality through the lens, and I was always stunned by the acuity of his eye: how he found the exact moment, the flash of unexpected beauty. For my part, I was practically incapable of taking a decent picture. I may as well have been blind. I borrowed his camera one time and the results were so bad that I gave up then and there. Not even phone filters could redeem them. My photos, unlike Zuri's, seemed to reduce reality, belittle it; the objects I photographed went flat, lost whatever charm they had had. I didn't even bother trying anymore. Why would I, if what my memory fell in love with was the whole gamut of impressions that different places sparked in me as I moved through them. Their density, the yellow light of a forest piercing particles of fog, the smell of charcoal kindled with Montezuma pine, the echo of footsteps down a long corridor roofed with vaulted herringbone brickwork, voices whispering secrets from one corner of a convent to another, the height of a wall, the weight of a roof, the damp in the shade, spontaneous words, water burbling in fountains, the brush of matter under the fingertips. Nothing that involved renouncing the passage of time.

We'd return to the city by evening and let the day fade out. We'd go to the mall and buy something frivolous, eat sushi, drink Oreo frappuccinos, nurse a beer to kill time – because we could only go to his place after eleven, when his mother would be in her bedroom or at her boyfriend's. As Zuri saw it, renting his own flat or living alone was just one among many things prevented by his condition. He couldn't last more than a couple of hours at my place or anywhere else. Going home with him was the only way we could spend the night together. The problem was that we had to sneak in like teenagers. I'd park in the street and he'd open the side door, taking care not to alarm the dogs. We'd make our way silently along the cobbled path that led to his room, which was annexed to the house but had a private entrance. The dogs always got worked up regardless: they'd bark furiously at me, and I always felt like they were about to snap at my legs.

Besides the hassle of the dogs, having to slink around and not being able to laugh out loud, we had a nice time in there. Sometimes we'd order pizza and watch TV series or just lie together under the covers, feet entwined, reading. We'd make love with pornographic exactitude, only in absolute silence. I'd learned my part, rehearsed my poses, and the act grew more and more precise, more and more natural. When we finished, we usually lay in silence for a long while as I brushed my fingers over the skin of his back and arms, almost without touching him, triggering a kind of electric charge, a tickle that made him tremble with longing. He'd stop me and I'd ask, are you all right? Then he'd ask me to keep going, and say I'd touch him gingerly this way until we fell asleep. The next day, I'd have to wake before dawn and sneak back out before the household stirred. I'd cut across the garden, freezing, as the dogs lunged at me with their toothy snouts. Of course it was humiliating to come and go like this, to hide from his family, but I persuaded myself it was necessary. I thought of how hard it must have been for him to secure any kind of autonomy, and I even felt flattered to have been admitted into the intimate universe he'd built behind the back of his childhood home. We were fine, really; as long as I adhered to those conditions, we could almost be a couple.

Our relationship went south when Rafita was named art director at the agency. Zuri complained that his boss was incompetent and that he was forced to clean up after him. He stopped taking his own photos and was always in a foul mood, rarely willing to give much of himself. I willingly compensated, as I had enthusiasm to spare; the difficult part was curbing my desire to give. I had to refrain from pouring my eagerness over his reserve, from interpreting his reserve as rejection, from taking his rejection as a snub whenever I sought him out or suggested we do something. Maybe that's why the invitation meant so much to me.

Rafita was throwing a housewarming party. The new apartment was a gift from his partner, the owner's nephew; he'd invited everyone from the office, and I urged Zuri to go. His boss was acting in good faith, and it was the perfect chance for them to reconcile. We talked about it over breakfast. He said he'd only go if I went with him, he was in no mood to make small talk with those people. It would be the first time we'd attended a group gathering of any kind, and I was excited to join his world, be his sidekick, wage the modest battle of social interaction together.

Rafita's new place was in one of those historical neighbourhoods where the mere presence of old stone buildings, Art Deco and bustling restaurants imbues the glass and concrete towers with gravitas. The architectural contrast was balanced out by an abundance of ash trees and jacarandas that had long spread their fronds and thickened their trunks. The building boasted an ironic, essentialist kind of luxury: soft lighting, polished cement surfaces, plaster walls intentionally scraped back to expose the brick below; black matte paint, moth-eaten wood, carefully appointed plants, broad balconies where the guests arranged themselves in clusters like figurines in a diorama.

I felt insecure as soon as a girl with cherry-coloured hair got into the lift with us. She looked utterly confident with her ripped trousers, her svelte form. She'd cut off the sleeves of her t-shirt to flaunt her tattoos, she wore no makeup and her hair was an unruly tangle, while I'd plaited mine, painted my eyes and lips and chosen a satin dress that made me look like a forty-something housewife. As if that weren't enough, I'd chosen a pair of heels I hadn't worn since my graduation party and they sliced into me as if I were walking on an endless bed of sharp stones. The girl said hello, pressed the button for the floor we were going to and stood in silence, studying the illuminated numbers, visibly smirking.

Rafita himself opened the door and leapt out to greet his friend with exaggerated euphoria. Meanwhile, I hugged my housewarming present – a potted rosemary plant – to my chest. What's that for? Zuri had asked when he saw me get out of the car with the plant. It's for your friend, I said tentatively. That idiot isn't my friend, he replied with deep, sincere contempt. Besides, he couldn't look after a rock. Rafita waved us in. I tried to give him the plant, but his response was forced: Thanks, just leave it there, and he brushed his hands together, not wanting to sully them with dirt. Then he gave us the tour of the flat: three bedrooms, three bathrooms, the one attached to the master bedroom has a classic bathtub, isn't it incredible, look, we call it the Marquess of Bath, isn't it gorgeous? And the two of us fit perfectly. We chose the tiles ourselves. The floors are pure cedar, lifetime guarantee. We'd looked at another place, a hundred and forty-three metres, but it had one of those laminated floors that never lasts, like that horrible plastic they used to put in poor people's houses, remember? Ugh, it felt so gross underfoot. Beers in the fridge, darling, thaaanks…

Suddenly I turned and couldn't find Zuri. Rafita was speaking in increasingly conspiratorial tones to the girl with the cherry-coloured hair; I felt like a third wheel. To keep from making a run for it, I took refuge in the kitchen. I held the rosemary plant under the tap, hoping the water would help it last a little longer. I left it in the sink beside a bag of ice, scraped a needle with my finger and sniffed it, convinced it was going to die. I took a beer from the fridge and went looking for Zuri, who was leaning against the far end of the balcony. He had a very full glass of Jack Daniel's in hand. He was talking with two co-workers and Linda Makina, the intern, who I recognised from her YouTube channel. I rested my back against the rail and sipped my beer.

The assistants were all young, good-looking, sure of themselves. They drank without their personalities becoming distorted by alcohol, laughed only when they were supposed to. Their emotional coldness contrasted with their extravagant clothing, hairstyles, haircuts, dye-jobs, tattoos, accessories. I, meanwhile, a flesh-and-blood ghost, couldn't figure out how to position my back so that the balcony railing wouldn't impale my ribs. I couldn't follow half of what they were saying: their vocabulary was bizarre, peppered with marketing terms, brand names, alien references, words in English. I didn't dare open my mouth for any reason other than to eat a couple of salmon and quark hors d'oeuvres. Zuri refilled his glass without even bothering to add ice this time. I would have gladly competed alongside him in the Jack Daniel's race, but I was driving and couldn't have more than a couple of beers.

On the other side of the glass door, in the white-furnished living room, a boyish girl with an undercut and large headphones bent over a console as she pieced together a retro playlist that no one appeared to be listening to. The men joked freely and didn't seem to notice the cleavage or bare legs of their female friends. Laughter like water splashing in a fountain. They were all so spontaneous, and I was intimidated by the theatrical ease of their conversation.

Zuri was on his fourth or fifth drink when Rafita re-joined the group. There was tension in their words and gestures, though I couldn't figure out why. Suddenly the tone escalated, and Zuri confronted his boss, glass in hand, slurring: You thick as shit motherfucker, he said, and I grabbed his arm to shut him up, but he yanked away, sloshing half his whisky down himself. Rafita's response was studiously indolent: You're embarrassing yourself, Zuri baby, go and drink some seltzer or something before you throw up all over the hardwood floors. Haughty, he turned away. The other two co-workers withdrew as well, while Linda Makina pursed her lips to keep from laughing.

I dragged Zuri toward one of the deck chairs on the balcony and asked the intern to stay with him while I got some water. When I came back, they were making out. I don't know what I felt most: furious, disappointed, fed up. I wanted to just leave him there, let him do whatever he wanted. But I couldn't. I knew he was spiralling. I planted myself right in front of them with an accusatory glare.

'Are you his sister?' the intern mumbled, vacant-eyed, hanging from Zuri's neck. 'You look like his sister.'

'What do you care. Get up,' I said, and when she did, I sat down in her place.

'We're leaving. Here, take this,' I told Zuri, placing the glass of water in his hands.

Linda Makina wasn't too far off the mark. More than his sister, I was like his nanny. I took him by the arm, helped him up and led him stumbling into the living room. I told him to wait for me to use the bathroom and left him leaning against the edge of the sofa. I peed and pulled my tights back up as quickly as I could. The cube-pattern floor tiles were smeared with mud and piss. As I re-emerged, I could hear a commotion. Nothing thunderous, a stirring at most, something that slightly exceeded the tone of everyday chatter. The slam of a door muffled by the air compressed around it. Rafita's face was frozen in a look of annoyance and his partner was murmuring he's a moron, don't even bother, forget it, come on. Zuri, of course, was no longer waiting by the sofa. Some of the guests glanced at me sidelong with a mix of pity and disapproval. Once again, I sought refuge in the kitchen while I gathered my strength to cross the hallway to the exit. By the time I reached the door, everyone had forgotten about us.

From the entrance to the building, I looked up and down the pavement. Zuri was sitting on the stoop of the building next door, staring at the ground, releasing a long plume of smoke. He didn't look up at the sound of my approaching steps, but when I stood in front of him and he saw me clutching the rosemary plant he flashed me a half-smile. He opened his rucksack and pulled out a bottle of Blue Label. My severance pay, he said smugly. I finally got them to fire me from that stupid fucking job, we have to celebrate. Unceremoniously, he opened the bottle right then and there, on the street: he peeled off the seal, snapped the ring, and tipped it sharply so that the liquid would stream into his throat.

It was only quarter past nine. We couldn't go to his house at that hour, nor could I drop him off there in such a state, so I brought him to my place. I opened the car door for him, undid his seatbelt, woke him up. I had to carry him up the stairs to the landing where the lift was. As soon as we were inside, he collapsed into bed on top of the rumpled blankets. I tossed my heels across the room, took off my satin dress, my bra, my stockings. My legs were swollen, and I felt thick, full of hormones. I went to the kitchen. I needed something strong and felt like I had the right to claim part of the spoils, so I poured myself a shot of Blue Label and gulped it down in an attempt to catch up. The liquor tasted heavy as caramel, and its perfume was different from ordinary Black, not to mention Red, far more intense; it settled somewhere behind my skull and gradually slackened my jaw and neck muscles with a feather-light touch. I put some music on my laptop, heated some leftover yakimeshi from the fridge and ate it as I scrolled through cat videos and other mindless content. I tried to roll a cigarette with Zuri's tobacco, but I couldn't get it as tight and uniform as he did. I lit it anyway. Someone like Koop or Françoise Hardy came on, and I could feel sorrow washing over me, accompanied by the old, familiar reproach of not being enough – of not ever being enough, not ever matching the measure of his desire, no matter how hard I tried.

It must have been past one by the time I dragged myself to bed. I felt sad and humiliated. I wanted to kick him out for the sake of my dignity, but what I wanted more than that was for him to love me, or at least acknowledge my place beside him. I considered what to tell him in the morning, how to clarify things, to find out what he wanted, what he was and wasn't willing to give. I hugged him from behind. Without fully waking, he turned over and pressed himself against me hard. His hands went straight for the fabric of my underwear. No, I said, wait, it's not the right time of the month. I didn't have a condom, I didn't want to, I wasn't in the mood. I tried to get him to look at me, but he was elsewhere, and I feared he'd get frustrated and storm out, feared I'd never see him again. So I let him find his way around the blankets and obstacles, let him make use of my body like an automaton, like someone who arrives home, opens the fridge and chugs juice right from the bottle. I surrendered. When he finished, I went to the bathroom to wash myself off between the legs, and when I came out I found him sitting on the edge of the mattress, tying his shoelaces, getting ready to leave.

'What are you doing?' I said. I asked him to stay, to hold me, please, just for a little while, but he said he had to go, and that was when I burst into tears. I tried to move closer, but his body was tense and he turned his face away. He made to leave. I leaned against the front door. I sat down on the floor, blabbering through hiccups. I asked him to forgive me for being who I am, made him promises that weren't in my power to keep. But instead of softening, he glared at me, exasperated, and locked himself in the bathroom. I poured myself another shot of Blue Label as I waited. I was standing in the doorway of the bedroom, clutching my glass, when I heard the rusty creak of the swinging window in the bathroom. He'd climbed on top of the toilet and slid his slender body through the air vent. I heard his footsteps on the patio, watched through the window in the door as his shadow headed for the lift, and then I could contain my rage no longer. I flung my drink against the glass so that the crash would express what was happening to me on the inside.

It was cold when I woke. The wind was blowing freely through the hole in the door, and the street noise sounded closer and clearer. I swallowed two Advils and got changed. Any neighbours who were up early that morning would catch sight of the chaos as they walked past: the empty bottle, clothes everywhere, papers, books, the full ashtray, the open laptop, the shards of glass on the ground. I collected the largest pieces and swept up the rest. I went down to the shop for a cardboard box to plug the hole, unfolded it, cut it down the middle, fixed it to the bars with masking tape. The box belonged to the Roma soap brand and the logo of the woman with plaited hair, washing clothes in a basin overflowing with bubbles, was upside-down. As I drank my coffee, I tried to reconstruct the events of the night before: the party at Rafita's house, the Blue Label, the ride home, the crying, the disarray, the fury, the glass hitting the window, the fright, the racket, the sense of humiliation that had cleaved to my memory like a splinter.

When I woke, the smell of ammonia brought back the day before and I thought of the house: what it would be like to strip off the flaking paint, repair the damaged areas with new plaster and paint it all white, scrape the old putty from the ironwork, replace the glass, trim the garden, plant vegetables, have the couch reupholstered, polish the parquet on the second floor and in the attic, pull up the carpets, vacuum the dust, throw out anything broken, sew new curtains. I checked my phone to see if Zuri had texted or called, but there was nothing. I put a pot of coffee on and went back to bed. I'd left the book of Perrault stories on the bedside table, an old, hardcover, cloth-bound edition with gold-embossed letters. The canvas spine was broken, the marbled flyleaf torn. It wouldn't be hard to fix. Doré's Bluebeard appeared on the cover: a big, whiskered fellow, hairy as a beast but bedecked with jewels, a lavish tunic and a top hat with an ostrich feather; he carried a mace and the key to a forbidden room with an expressive look of warning on his face; he gazed bulge-eyed at the fragile maiden with a discreet profile who in turn couldn't tear her eyes from the key, almost taking it into her hands, engrossed, blind to the monstrosity before her. I was about to start reading when I heard someone rapping on the metal doorframe. I knew that summons, and I would have recognised the silhouette beyond the windowpane, too, if there hadn't been a Roma soap box there instead of glass. I glanced around my messy, ammonia-infused flat. The manager knocked again, but I lay still under the covers. Then I heard him slip a piece of paper through the crack, his footsteps fading across the patio. I got out of bed and went to pick it up. It was a memo on the estate agent's letterhead. This letter serves to inform you… disturbances, property damage, substance abuse, complaints from the neighbours… contract number… which expires on… will not be renewed, and you must vacate the premises by… I folded the document and fanned myself with it as I thought again about the house and the possibility of restoring it. Maybe Zuri would rent me one of the rooms as remuneration: two birds with one stone.

I rinsed the jar for the last time. I should have used gloves; my hands stung. I turned it over to dry on a towel on the patio. I sat down beside it like someone waiting by an oven for bread to bake, then finally opened the book to read. When the young woman entered the first room, she saw that everything was made of gold: the window frames, the bedposts, the floor, the moulding on the walls, the mirrors, the cups and glasses; the trunks contained heaps of pure gold coins; the wardrobes, decorated with gold estofado inside and out, were bursting with dresses embroidered with golden thread, gold shoes, gold wigs, gold jewellery; even the letter-writing paper was streaked with golden fibres, and the content of the heavy inkwell was liquid gold.

Zuri called around four. He asked about the vase. I said yes, I have it here, I brought it home to clean it, it's actually time to remove the paste. I glanced at the clock.

I'll pick it up, he said. I felt instantly rattled: the flat was a disaster and still reeked of ammonia. I'll be there in twenty minutes, he added, and hung up. I tidied a little, hid the box from the pizza I'd ordered and hurried to rub the paste off with the flannel. Every filigree gave off new light and the cobalt blue looked like fresh ink.

When I heard the doorbell, it dawned on me that I hadn't showered and was still wearing my pyjamas. I lifted the receiver and heard him say hi, it's me. I buzzed him in and ran to the bathroom, stood briefly under the stream without waiting for the water to heat up. I left the door open so I could hear him come in. I'll be out in a minute, I yelled. I finished rinsing the shampoo out of my hair, turned off the water, and wrapped myself in a towel.

'Sorry about the smell. It's the cleaning product.'

'It's fine, it doesn't bother me,' he answered from the living room. 'Do you know where I can buy flowers at this time of day? I stopped at the grocery store, but they were out, and the florist was closed.'

'Hmm, let me think.'

I put on some underwear, deodorant, tried to tame my hair.

'I got into a fight with Patricia.' That's what he called his mother. 'She doesn't want Don Eligio's ashes in our house, I'll have to take them to his. Come with me?'

'Of course,' I said, pulling on any old t-shirt.

I hadn't understood that we were talking about a funeral until I entered the living room and saw him dressed in a black shirt and suit. I remember feeling enthralled by the aura of pensive, existentialist dandy the outfit gave him. I'll just be a minute, I said, and ran to swap my trousers and t-shirt for a dark red velvet dress, ballerina-style, with a tie-strap bustier, fishnet stockings and lace-up ankle boots. I sprayed myself with perfume, put on lipstick. When I finally came out, Zuri was studying the blue lines on the porcelain. I hugged him from behind.

'This sign over here is *kuài* and this one is *tiān*. They mean something like the beginning and the end.'

He raised his eyebrows in surprise and turned to look at me.

'Wow, you look really nice,' he said, and I felt complete.

I wrapped the vase in a clean cloth and tucked it into a bag. I took my handbag, a pashmina, my keys and a pair of scissors, then went out to cut some flowers for a bouquet: three lilies, six hibiscus blossoms, a yellow rosebud, a handful of red lantanas and another handful of purple ones to flesh out the base. Zuri waited testily at the end of the ramp. You're crazy, not those, he said when he grasped my intentions. As if flowers had to be bought from a florist to be worthy. The house was a few streets away from my place. He carried the bag with the vase inside and the urn of Don Eligio's ashes in his rucksack. The park was quiet at that hour. The slate-grey sky was beginning to solidify the shadows, but I knew where to look. Making sure there weren't any security guards around, I slipped into the bushes in search of the offering. Theft successful, I emerged onto the path, climbed the ramp and re-joined Zuri with a triumphant smile. He smiled too, purse-lipped, rolling his eyes and shaking his head. He took out his pouch of tobacco and we leaned against the wall. It was incredible how quickly and deftly he could roll a cigarette, like a magician. The lighter flame consumed the tip. I reached out for a drag and asked him, after a long exhalation: Are you serious? Do you really want me to help you restore the house?

We approached the corner gate in a different mood, eager, making plans. Zuri needed the space clean and functional in less than three months. He wanted to set up his studio in the attic, clear the living room for a gallery and clean the bedrooms in case they could be rented as offices or he, or we, could live in them. It was the first time he'd ever suggested something like this and I couldn't help but startle, though I managed to keep my cool. Maybe it was the thrill of the moment that had led him to propose such a thing. I didn't want to get my hopes up.

We walked over the dead leaves, circling the construction, studying the details of the façade. Diagnosing quickly, based on what I'd seen the day before, I told him that the structure was well preserved, it looked stable, though we ought to have an architect evaluate it regardless. It needed a full inspection, scraping back the stucco, weatherproofing, a deep clean. It seemed to me that the most difficult part would be getting rid of all the junk, figuring out what to do with each and every object. You can junk it all, as far as I'm concerned, he told me. All he wanted were the books, the documents, and anything related to his trade. I'd need to draw up a reasonably detailed proposal, complete with dates, costs and a breakdown of what I'd charge, for his aunt Silvia and the lawyers, so that they could come up with a stipend and reach an agreement. Although, in truth, I was willing to do it even if he didn't pay me, even if I had to pay out of my own pocket. In that moment, I would have done anything to be able to build a life by his side.

It was the time of day when the shadows began to grow inside the house. I tried to turn on a light, but it didn't work, and I deduced there was no power. Zuri wanted to be quick about things, to take the vase and urn up to the attic as soon as possible and set them beside each other as he'd been instructed. He made straight for the stairs, but I asked him to wait while I went and got a white glass kerosene lamp I'd seen on the mantlepiece. I held the lamp up to the light to make sure it had enough fuel. I removed the bulb with great care and cleaned off the dust with an old napkin. The wick was coated in fluff, but it hadn't dried out. Zuri handed me his lighter and the flame sketched a blue circle that brightened the room and allowed us to breathe more easily. Next to the chimney was a well-stocked drinks trolley: rum, gin, whisky. Zuri wasted no time in checking the labels. He selected one called Longrow, uncapped it, sniffed the contents. Safe, he said. I reinserted the bulb into the base and we made our way upstairs on a surer footing.

We walked down the hall, past its six doors and through the room with the Chinese furniture. We climbed the straight flight of stairs to the attic. There was no lingering trace of the smell. We set our cargo on the ground and, with no glasses to hand, took long swigs of Longrow right from the bottle. We improvised a kind of altar by the arched windows: a Louis XV griffin-foot console table against the wall and a mirror with a gold-volute frame resting on the tabletop. The animated light from the kerosene lamp shone on the rusty quick-silver and the lunar markings granted the reflection a dreamlike, memorious air. Zuri rummaged in the trunk for a photo of his uncle. I took the vase out of the bag and placed it in the centre, the life sign facing outward, the death sign reflected in the mirror. I laid the flowers on the left. Zuri extracted the urn from his backpack and held it for a few moments, pensive and still, before he positioned it beside the vase. Eligio Vargas Pani (1933–2015). Finally, he leaned the photograph against the urn: it showed a young, thin, fair-skinned man with very thick eyebrows. There was an indisputable family resemblance. Don Eligio was smoking a cigarette, wearing a hat and a coat with a turned-up collar. He had a Hasselblad camera in his hands. The image captured his reflection in the window of a photography supply store. Strange, I thought, an old-school selfie.

'Don't you want to say a few words?' I asked.

'No, I just need to leave the ashes here for now. We'll have a ceremony in three months, when the house is ready and guests can come.'

We sat down on the ottoman and began to drink as we made plans for the house, for the near future. Zuri would travel to Chicago to sort out the inheritance paperwork with his aunt, study the cameras his uncle had left him and practise so he could start to work with them. Meanwhile, he'd continue with his commissions, wrap up ongoing commitments and start networking in hopes of setting up a gallery. The house was the most important part of the whole plan, and it depended on me.

The Longrow bottle was more than halfway gone by the time we started to kiss, stretched out on the ottoman. There was something different about him. His touch was contemplative, unrushed, without the kind of desire that seeks instant satisfaction. The change had the opposite effect on me. Desperate, I unbuckled his pants and sought his sex, a slim, tender mouthful I tongued like candy until I felt the shuddering flesh expand into the soft confines of my mouth. I hiked up my dress and sat astride him to sate my other mouth, soaked and hungry. He filled me, harder and deeper with every thrust, the rhythm intensifying. We changed positions a couple of times. He got up and crouched behind me, his knees on the edge of the ottoman, hands on the ledge, the corolla of my dress splayed open like a poppy to receive a stinger, a bee determined to detonate the violent beat of blood. Afterwards, we drowsed, his member still inside me, his body resting languidly against mine. I reached out for the blanket I'd used to wrap the vase and draped it over us. Zuri settled beside me and succumbed so profoundly that the tremors of his dream didn't wake him.

I woke before dawn. Zuri was still sleeping at my side. I closed my eyes to treasure the moment, savour my joy. My head felt clear, and in this clarity I heard the first birdsong of the day. Before long I got up and went to the window: I saw people walking to the park with their dogs, running, heading to work. It was Monday, I had to go to the Institute, but there was time. The vague aspiration of restoring and inhabiting this house had abruptly become a concrete plan. I needed coffee. I looked for my underwear and zipped Zuri's jacket over my dress, grabbed my bag and went downstairs. I left the front door and the gate slightly ajar. I took one look at the house before turning my back on it and making my way to the coffee shop. I felt infatuated: a tender new leaf, bright with sun and dew.

I ordered two lattes, a cranberry coconut bun for Zuri, and a lemon cookie for myself, the one with the thickest coating of powdered sugar. I returned with the cups in a cardboard carrier, the pastries in a bag. Back at the house, I stopped in the front hall. The pale light shimmered on the window panes. I sat down on the stairs, not caring if my dress got dirty. I took a sip of coffee: still too hot. I tried to be realistic. How difficult would it be, where should we start. By getting rid of all the junk, that much was clear.

On the back of a flyer for a pest control company, I made a list and some rough calculations: a builder, the material, the waste removal, the permits. I pictured myself in gloves and a facemask, hair tied back with a kerchief, moving furniture, taking out the rubbish, cleaning. The very thought of rectifying such neglect was satisfying to me. Maybe we could hold a garage sale and sell some trinkets to help with expenses, or put together a whole lot and pitch it to a collector. The plaster repairs could be tackled in sections, as could the interior and exterior paint jobs, the carpentry, the garden, the finishings, the decorations. I pictured Zuri's photos printed in large format, hung on white walls. Cocktails, receptions, book launches, parties, an office. It delighted me that Zuri was taking his profession seriously at last, devoting himself to making new work, forgetting about the agencies and commissions that had always drained him. All I needed was for him to let me occupy one of the second-floor bedrooms so I could set up a workshop, a drafting table, my tools, plenty of open space. The plan was perfect, timely for both of us, practically speaking, and convenient for me, in the sense that we'd be close without him feeling overwhelmed by the pressure of norms and commitments. I knew I'd have to be cautious, curb my intensity, be professional. Of course, it would take a lot of money and a lot of work, especially work; to inhabit a space is to appropriate it through lovingly repeated acts. But so what: love was what I had in spades.

I hear the click, light carving up time. I feel the weight of his gaze through the lens. I touch the smooth, cold marble surface as I pick up the three Chinese coins, feel their solidity in my palm. I look down to avoid the flash. I shake the coins, toss them for the second time. Clink and spin. The game of probabilities is determined. Two yins, one yang. I draw the second solid line above the first split one. Yang: repair what was damaged by the mother.

The woman crumples to the floor, under the dining room table. She smooths the fabric of her skirt to cover her knees. Her hair is tangled, her face splattered with black paint. Right in the middle of the living area, between the lounge, dining room and chimney, she spies one of her high-heeled shoes: beige calfskin adorned with delicate folds on the bridge, in the style of León, Guanajuato. Abandoned there, it looks like a distant, unreachable object, as if it already belonged to another time, synecdoche of itself.

The woman breathes in and out, tries not to cry. Her wide eyes peer around the chair legs at the feet of the two men making their way towards the door.

'I adore *Turandot* – I can't believe I've still never seen it live,' says one, opening the door to let the other through. She can see their sharp-edged shadows on the floor of the front hall.

'It's stunning!' the other says. 'And best of all, they brought in Wang Kun. You'll get goosepimples when you hear the first notes of *In questa reggia*' – the voice starts to sing – '*or son mill'anni e mille, un grido disperato risonò*' – they shut the door. '*E quel grido, traverso stirpe e stirpe…*'

One of the men hangs a small key on a hook before he goes. The voice drifts away, singing *enigmi sono tre, la morte è una...* and the house is submerged in silence once more. All she can hear is a flutter, the shadow of a wing beating against the windows: a moth dashes itself to pieces as it strains to reach the light.

I slapped my hands on my legs before getting up and returning, resolute, to the attic. Zuri was still asleep. I left the cups and pastries on the lid of the trunk and lay down beside him again. I stroked his hair, kissed him on the temple. I brought coffee and one of those buns you like, I said. He opened his eyes and stretched. He looked confused, as if he were suddenly ashamed to find himself there. He sat up on the ottoman and I placed the cup in his hands. Careful, it's probably still hot. He took a sip and stared vacantly at a specific spot on the ground, rubbed his face with his palms.

What we talked about yesterday is still on, right? He turned to look at me as if he'd become aware of the present only then, only then realised I was there with him, and he said yes, of course, please, go ahead and take care of everything. I know I can trust you. Here – he handed me the keys – all yours. All I ask is that you be very careful with the photography equipment. Otherwise you can do whatever you want. Throw away whatever you need to throw away and sell whatever you want to sell. I imagine you'll have to hire some people. Any idea how much you'll need to get started? I passed him the calculations I'd made. Good, he said, you can start anytime, and I'll deposit the money as soon as everything's settled up there.

He got dressed, downed the coffee, took a bite of the bun and gathered his things. We went downstairs together. He was flying to Chicago the following Saturday, so we probably wouldn't be seeing each other for a while, two or three weeks. At the bottom of the stairs, I gave him a hug and told him how much I cared about him, that I was grateful for the chance to do this together. He kissed me lightly, tasting of coffee and goodbyes. He paused in the doorway, then turned: One important thing, he said. Don't open the door to the little store room at the back of the house. The key's on the hook, but don't go in for any reason, please. My uncle's things are in there, something could get ruined, OK? I nodded and told him not to worry, if he told me not to open that door, I wouldn't, end of story. Zuri smiled for the last time and stepped out. I stood in the doorway, then sat on the stoop and watched him walk away in the time it took for the house's shadowy embrace to settle around my shoulders. I nearly suffocated with the joy of having it all. I felt the metal spikes of the keys in my palm. I didn't want to open my fingers to look. They say dreams dissolve when you look at your hands.

'Neocolonial architecture is a farce, a pastiche, and if you catch me in a bad mood, I'll tell you it's a bona fide betrayal,' said Dr Juaresantana in Real Estate Restoration class. 'Those of you who made it through primary school will remember that in the years following the Revolution, all kinds of politicians and intellectuals were desperate to restore a sense of national identity, although at the time no one had any idea what the hell "national" even meant. Huitlacoche, embroidered blouses from Tehuantepec, regional dances, those dreadful, ear-splitting mariachi trumpets, and, of course, the aberration known as "California Colonial".' The first slide showed a mansion in the Polanco neighbourhood of Mexico City. Her habit of continually confronting us with unresolvable paradoxes had earned Dr Emilia Juárez Santillana the nickname Juaresantana (pronounced by her students as a single word), after nineteenth-century presidents Juárez and Santa Anna, famous for pulling the country in conflicting directions. For an hour and a half, she would convince us that Porfirio Díaz had been a true hero of urban planning, then oust him from his pedestal with a single blow: 'Of course his taste for Frenchified architecture didn't spare him from being a classist pig and a vicious dictator, and the resulting socio-urban disasters were x and y.' She knew about her nickname and disliked it, but it didn't offend her: 'I'm going to pretend it's because of Carlos Santana.'

'During his mandate', she went on, 'sometime in the 1920s, Carranza decreed a tax exemption for any building projects that incorporated elements of national identity, which meant: cantera stone, terracotta, tile, balconies and alcoves. As you can see' – she clicked to a slide of the National Palace – 'this wasn't so bad when it came to public buildings, because it meant tourists started coming to Mexico to ooh and ahh over the so-called City of Palaces, even though the façades are warped and wonky as corn chips. Residential buildings are another story. For starters, the construction of ridiculous extravagances like this one' – she showed another mansion in Lomas de Chapultepec – 'at a time when the country was going to the dogs, is unequivocal proof that we got off on the wrong foot, that inequality was as bad then as it is now, or even worse.

'Another important thing: remember that function-alism was starting to take off, the novelty of a house with integrated utilities, where you didn't have to go outside to the latrine or to do the laundry or cook on the fire. And so, to placate the socialites of the day, while exalting so-called national features to justify tax exemptions, canny architects imported the Hollywood trend for Spanish-style mansions, gussied them up with baroque ornaments and other frills, which have always come naturally to us Mexicans, and voilà: California Colonial. It was like getting re-conquered by the Spanish, but with a gringo twist, with baroque Catholic embellishments and Art Deco modular smoothness thrown in just for the hell of it,' she quipped sardonically.

'The interiors, which are almost always sober in design, are like a Pedro Infante movie set: staircases with balustrades, lots of stories, lots of balconies, lots of skylights, turned wooden furniture and high-ceilinged rooms that look like Sara García might appear at any moment. Basically, a Frankenstein's monster that has nonetheless been legitimised over time. They may be ugly mashups and then some, but they're still the last of those era-defining mansions, and they defend the urban landscape against politicians' palaces, Santa Fe's glass monstrosities, multi-family complexes, and social housing slums.'

After another twenty images and a round of questions and answers, Dr Juaresantana had the last word: 'California Colonial is a good example of our limitations as architects, kids. But just because it's a pastiche that reminds us of the own goal of nationalism and Mexico's identity crisis, does that mean we should tear these buildings down, like they're doing in Tequisquiapan, in San Luis Potosí? No, sir: it's not our job to judge the legitimacy of history. It's our job to preserve and restore it.'

I was still sitting on the steps at the front of the house when I heard the sound of a broom. First it was a distant, almost imperceptible murmur, but it gradually grew closer and clearer. It couldn't be coming from the street, no one was sweeping there; it had to be in the back garden. I got up and followed the circular path until I reached the thickets and patches of unkempt weeds skirting the enclosing wall and the sides of the house. An old woman was the one doing the sweeping. She was wearing a speckled shawl and an apron embroidered with flowers, her white plaits tied with a ribbon down her back. I called out, then moved closer when she didn't hear me at first. She looked up and serenely raised a hand in greeting. I told her apologetically that I didn't know anyone had been looking after the house. She swept on in silence. I explained that I'd been hired to restore the house, but she didn't respond to that, either. I asked if she was part of the family, if she lived there, if I was intruding by showing up to work there, if my presence would interfere with her tasks.

'It's alright, it's alright, child, I understand,' she said at last. 'I just stop by to tidy up, when I can.'

'I'm very glad to meet you. What's your name?'

'Oralia.'

'Did you know the family who used to live here?'

'I've worked for them since I was sixteen years old, imagine that. And I can't tell you how hard it's been to keep the house in order...'

'Well, now you'll have someone to lend you a hand, Doña Oralia.'

I knelt to pick up the pile of leaves between two pieces of cardboard and drop them into the bucket.

'Leave that, child, you'll get your dress dirty.'

'It's filthy already, don't worry about that,' I reassured her, and went on collecting the leaves.

'By the way', she said, leaning her weight on the broom, 'the power switch is behind the door.'

'I'm sorry?'

'There is power, you just have to flick the switch behind the door,' she said, and continued sweeping towards the path. I thanked her. I wondered if she knew that Don Eligio had died, but I didn't want to meddle.

I finished with the leaves, and only then realised that the sound of the broom had gone. So had Oralia. I went into the house and looked for the mains switch in the spot she'd described. The electrical panel looked intact. Just to test it, I lifted the levers and heard the distant purring of the water pump filling the tank in response. I scolded myself for not having tried it earlier, although it was a real relief, one less thing to deal with. I flicked the switches down again and the house resumed its silence. I went out, closed the door, shut the gate, and headed for the main road, my mind overflowing with hopes and plans.

TWO

CHIMAERA

For the second photo, you ask me to stand naked at the window. Your voice sounds slightly deeper than usual. I refuse to look at you for fear of discovering you're actually a stranger, but you come over and one of the lamps illuminates your face. I peer into the shadows. I feel like someone else is watching, though we're alone in the attic. You pick up the red book and show me the symbol on the cover, an ideogram formed by two strokes like the open legs of an A, a horizontal line above them like the arms of a pentagram and an accent mark above that. You ask me to breathe on the glass until it steams up, then draw the symbol with my index finger.

I practice the figure several times on my palm. I try to shake off my shyness as I slip off the delicate white muslin dressing gown. Then I take off my knickers too and go to the window. I watch you press your eye to the camera's viewfinder, studying the shot. Meanwhile, I've got goosebumps from the cold – I can see my hairs standing on end and my nipples are hard and tight like the golden peak of a muffin. I feel a faint tremor at the centre of my body. You take your time changing the film, adjusting the lamps and reflectors. It can't be easy to take a photo in front of a window when it's dark outside. I turn and rest my naked buttocks on the windowsill. I try to cover my breasts with my arms.

'What's the novel about?' I ask, to distract myself from the cold, to get your attention.

'Which novel?'

'This one, the one the photos are from.'

'It's…' You go to the table for the photometer and bring it into the perimeter of light, read the numbers, move one of the lamps back a bit. 'It's not really about anything specific.'

'What do you mean?'

'It's like a whole bunch of images that come together, but nothing actually happens.'

'How can nothing happen? It's a novel.'

'I mean, things happen, but hypothetically, like variations on a single image, and what we're representing here are those variations…'

You signal that you're ready, I turn and breathe on the glass until it steams up.

'Let's say it's, like, a visual interpretation of the novel's factuality', you say, your finger suspended over the shutter.

'What do you mean its factuality, if supposedly nothing happens?'

I draw the ideogram in the mist on the window. I drag the tip of my index finger over the damp surface, the three strokes and the horizontal line: a five pointed star. I hear your steady breathing behind me, the click of the shutter. In the photograph, the line of my shoulder will be silhouetted against the dark glass. The branches of the tulip tree dip their flowers into the night's heavy sky. My face and breasts are reflected on the windowpane. I imagine someone hiding down there, watching me from the undergrowth, someone in the street watching a naked woman lean against the sill, drawing a Chinese ideogram on the steamed-up window, even though it's raining and I doubt anyone is out walking in this weather.

'Do you remember the photo from the trunk?'

'The one of the man being cut to pieces?'

'Yeah.'

'You're not going to cut me to pieces, are you?'

'Don't be ridiculous, Min, it'll be a representation, obviously. A photomontage, with stage effects and fake blood.'

'Uh oh, now I'm getting nervous again.'

'Just bear with me, I need one last series...'

A sudden gust of wind flings open the door and slams it against the wall, and I spin round, hunched over, covering my breasts and pubis, my face full of shock and shame.

The coins fall on the same side, three yangs make a yang, nine on the third toss. I draw a solid line beneath the two previous broken ones: signs of strife and a faint cause for regret.

The first bedroom was tidy and peaceful, suspended in silence. Although the furniture belonged to a wedding set, the room had an overwhelmingly female touch: the dressing table by the doorway, the four-poster bed facing west, the nightstands on either side, each bearing a lamp with a silk lampshade, a full-length mirror in a back corner and two armchairs by the French doors looking out onto the balcony. The blush-coloured carpet muted the sound of my footsteps. Thick clumps of dust and wool had gathered in the corners among the pieces of gaudy jewellery, on the satin pillows and at the foot of the curtains that matched the carpet and flowery wallpaper, among the bottles of perfume and pots of cream lined up in front of the dressing table mirror, on the lacquer jewellery box from Michoacán, among the hairbrushes, little tubes and hairpins, in the basket of brooches and combs and make-up brushes, among the eyeshadow palettes and the lipsticks, on the box of mini Maja soaps with their haughty looking flamenco dancer on the back, the mother-of-pearl compact mirror, the rosary and the open packet of Parisienne cigarettes with a metal floral patterned lighter hidden inside.

On the corner of the dresser there was a worn-out, metal-beaded coin purse, packed with old notes and coins, a bus ticket, a key and some mints. The jewellery box was full of pearls and fake jewels in elaborate period designs. I picked up an enormous earring set with multi-coloured rhinestones, hideous and heavy. When I clipped it on, I felt my pulse beat painfully in my earlobe. I took it off at once. I opened an eyeshadow palette shaped like a peacock's tail: each feather held a different coloured powder. I rubbed the tip of my finger on the pink, applied the iridescent colour to my cheeks and laughed at a sudden memory of playing with my mother's things behind her back. I remembered her rough hands scrubbing at my face under the tap. The perfumes were rancid by now, but the bright red butter of the lipsticks was still very soft.

It was clear that the room hadn't been touched since the moment the door was closed, although time had continued to pass for the objects inside, dust particles pulsing slowly, matter crumbling away. The natural thing would have been for the objects to scatter around the world, for the dresses to be released one by one in search of their fortune, for the coats to be given away or passed down, for the high heels to make way for more sober, comfortable shoes, an older lady's moccasins, slippers. If the house had been abandoned due to illness, there would be signs, however faint, of convalescence. But there were no medications among the perfumes, nor did the mattress look like anyone had been bed-bound there. It was as though the bedroom's occupant had simply left one day, just kept walking until she disappeared; no purse, no bag, no suitcase, no travelling clothes, no toiletries. As though, by closing that door, someone had also slammed shut her whole life.

The wardrobe ran the length of the wall opposite the bed. It had an intense, sharply human scent that mingled with the smell of leather and damp. The shoes were drowning in a sea of fluff that the clothes had gradually shed like flakes of skin. Dresses languished in plastic bags, fabrics with red, orange and brown prints, black and avocado green, ochre, burnt orange, lime green. Some tended towards the psychedelic; others were more elegant and conservative, Chanel-style cuts in thick, plain fabrics, but with sturdy textures that time hadn't damaged in the least. The final third of the rack was occupied by coats in different leathers – I couldn't have named the prey animals they'd come from, but some still had tails and taxidermied heads. Horrible as they were, my hands couldn't resist: I took the first one down off its hanger. I felt its animal weight around my shoulders, a languid embrace, the gentlest touch around my neck, the smell of hide and the faint trace of a perfume and a body long gone. In the wardrobe's various compartments were all manner of opulent accessories, sunglasses, silk neckerchiefs, gloves, hats, veiled fascinators, wallets that matched the shoes. I needed something to cover my head and keep the dust out of my hair. From among the silks in the top drawer I chose a simple bandana. I brought a footstool over and tugged at the cloth, but one of its corners was stuck. When I put my hand in, I discovered the edge was trapped down the back of the drawer, resisting when I pulled. The mechanism was very simple: press and release. I pushed aside the jumble of scarves and gloves – and that was how I discovered the false bottom that concealed the safe. I turned the knob, just to check it was locked. I imagined Zuri's relatives would give him the combination, but I was dying to see what was inside. Maybe I could even crack the code myself, then tell him about it and show him the untouched contents as proof of my integrity.

I took the bandana and put the other things back where they were. I looked at the dresses again. They were more or less my size, though I was surprised at how accentuated the waists were, as though women used to be shaped differently, cut to the mould of the flesh-coloured corsets and shapewear made back in the day; there was an entire drawer of them. I looked at myself in the mirror, holding a black dress against my body, and then a different lime-coloured one, and a Chanel suit with spongy shoulder pads. I undressed in front of my reflection, delighted at the chance to pretend I was someone else. I threw my clothes on the bed and tried the first one on.

The woman pulled her stockings up to her thighs and clipped the hems in place. The nylon slip she'd dropped to the mattress slipped over the edge and onto the diamond patterned skirt and brown jumper tangled together on the floor. She put on a cream pencil skirt and an organza blouse, but the outfit had no contrasts, it was like a spoonful of meringue. She changed into the black pleated skirt but thought the length didn't suit her. She tried on a flowery dress, but it was too modest, the guests would be cultured, sophisticated, and she didn't want to look like a country girl, a mere housewife. She tried on a tailored suit but felt hot as soon as the wool touched her skin. She tried on an evening gown, but the shimmer of the beaded embroidery seemed excessive for a dinner in her own home. She returned to the organza blouse, this time unbuttoned at the neck, a black pencil skirt and black heels. She smiled at her own reflection. The outfit was discreet, but it showed off her figure, which she'd worked so hard to get back after the twins. She went to the dressing table and picked up the hairpiece, secured it with pins, sorted out the weft at the back of her neck and applied more perfume to her wrists and neck. Finally, a touch of bright red lipstick.

She'd been in the kitchen when the doorbell rang, still looking a mess, wearing that diamond patterned skirt and her old brown jumper with the sleeves rolled up to her elbows like a schoolgirl; over it she'd tied the ugliest, dirtiest apron, scorched down one side. She shouted to Oralia to get the door, but she didn't seem to hear – she was probably still putting the girls to bed. The doorbell went again. She went into the dining room to call Oralia a second time, or so that Eligio, who had locked himself in the library, would figure out that they were both busy and do them the favour of answering the door. The asparagus soup reached the rim of the saucepan and she ran back, spoon in hand, to keep it from boiling over. It was very early, the guests weren't due for another half an hour, but the doorbell had rung, no doubt about it. The soup hadn't fully thickened yet and she still had to go upstairs and change. A figure darkened the window and the mosquito screen squeaked on its hinges.

'Oh, you've arrived! How embarrassing, I'm sorry, here I am with my hands full and God only knows where that girl's got to… Oralia!'

The man came over, smiling. He had a bottle of wine in one hand and a second one in his pocket. His hair was neatly slicked and he wore a white handkerchief in his lapel.

'It smells delicious in here! What's on the menu?' His voice was slightly nasal.

'I've made stuffed pork loin with cherry sauce and a Russian salad.' She was still stirring the white foam. 'Prawn ravioli and asparagus soup to start. Oh, and chocolate cake for dessert.'

'Gató-chocolá! Delicious!'

'What did you call it?'

'Sorry, *gâteau au chocolat*', he pronounced more correctly.

'Oh yes, *gâteau* …'

'Oh, *parlez-vous…*?'

'No, of course not. I learned about three words at school, that's all.'

'Well as it turns out, gató-chocolá is my favourite dessert… especially with a ripe blackberry compote…'

'Oh! I didn't know people ate it with blackberries. What an unusual combination.'

'You must try it, dear! *C'est une exquisité.*' He leaned over the pan and breathed in. 'May I?'

Noting his hand still tucked in his pocket, the woman lifted the wooden spoon and blew. The spoonful of creamed asparagus rippled, steaming. Then she held it unsteadily to his mouth. The man's face lit up at the taste.

'Would you like to try the pork loin? It's a family recipe.' She turned off the stove and opened the oven door to see how it was doing.

'Honestly, I'd prefer the ravioli. I'm not keen on loin, I find it too dry, it's, I don't know, *très épicé…* Speaking of which, I brought a bottle of wine. It ought to be good, because it was in my father's cellar.' He laughed like a mischievous child. She handed him the corkscrew and went to the sideboard for a glass.

When she returned, he'd opened the bottle and pulled the cork off the corkscrew. He poured a little wine, swirled it against the walls of the glass and thrust his nose in, a gesture she found grotesque and disconcerting. Sticking his nostrils all the way inside like that, instead of tasting it? He seemed satisfied and immediately offered her the glass.

'They say it's good luck for the first toast to be in the kitchen.'

She accepted the glass and clinked it against the bottle he held up with a ceremonious flourish. She touched her lips to the rim as he watched her carefully. They laughed. She tasted the liquid and was surprised to realise it was the best wine she'd ever tasted. She passed him the glass and he took a sip too.

'Not bad,' he said.

'What do you mean, it's delicious! But can you get this here?' she asked, animated, her face shining.

'I doubt it, my dear. All my father's wines are imported. This is a '45 Bordeaux, it's probably worth a fortune. But why don't we do this.' He skewered the cork again. 'The French like to drink while they're cooking – perhaps that's where they get their *bon goût*. I'm going to leave this bottle right here, safely out of sight' – he tucked it away beside the fridge – 'so only you and I know it's there, and if you'll allow me, I'm going to pour myself a gin, because the truth is I need something stronger. I expect Eligio's in the library, is he…?'

Oralia appeared as the man headed towards the living room and the little trolley bearing spirits, glasses, ice and tonic water. She hid the glass of wine beside the bottle and instructed the young woman to add the final touches to the dinner: take out the pork in ten minutes, finish off the gratin for the ravioli, put the Russian salad in a glass serving dish and the asparagus soup in the tureen. Then she went into the pantry and started searching. She had the vague sense that somewhere, deep among the shelves, there was a forgotten vase of blackberry jam.

The coins indicate that the fourth line is yang: the past begins to reveal itself and the individual, instead of taking measures, allows decay to run its course.

I returned to the house the next morning. After all the time I'd spent thinking about it, imagining it restored to its former glory, I practically belonged to it now. I cut across the park, and as I went up the ramp I could make out the roof tiles among the treetops. It was June, and not cold, though the vegetation kept the air cool, because it had rained the night before and the ground was damp, the pavements dyed green, the bushes heavy with dew. A shiver of responsibility ran through me, much like the one I felt when my mother first sent me to the market alone, armed with a bag, money and a list. Now I was to restore a building by myself for the first time. I crossed the street, opened the gate, took the three stairs and fitted the key into the front lock. I was about to open it when I realised someone was watching me. From the window of a pickup parked on the corner, a young man was following my movements, attentive and curious. His face looked familiar. So did his pickup. I set down my bag of provisions and went over.

The young man was dark-skinned and thin, though he had a round face. His truck, a faded old red Ford, had a metal structure over the back shaped like a house with a gabled roof, which was covered with a blue tarpaulin that spelled out in large letters: 'Gutiérrez Freight and Removals', followed by a telephone number and a slogan: 'Experts in Fragile Items'. I thought I'd seen it before. I used to see it parked round the corner from the Institute and it reminded me of Máicol, my father's trusty removals guy, who marketed himself with the slogan 'Homes Delivered'. People laughed, but the joke proved to be effective publicity and business took off so much that he set up his own company and stopped coming round anymore. I went over to the window. The man turned down the news on the radio and we said hello.

'You're the one who parks in front of the church, right?' I recognised his Raiders cap, the pirate's face over two crossed cutlasses.

'That's right. Can I help with anything?' He took the keys out of the ignition and got out of the pickup.

'We're going to be working on this house.' I used a defensive plural, just in case, and gestured with my thumb over my shoulder. 'I might need you to make a few trips in the truck.'

'Of course, just tell me when and where.' He studied the façade.

'Thanks, let me write down your number. I'll call you, tomorrow maybe, or I'll come and find you round here. We'll be getting rid of a lot of junk, so we'll need help lugging stuff out…'

'Whatever you need, just let us know.'

'What's your name?'

'Mario.'

'OK, Mario, I'm going to get everyone started here, but let's be in touch,' I said, as though I really was in charge and had people working for me.

I saved his number and said goodbye. He seemed

reliable, and in the end, there was always a sense of trust among people from the same neighbourhood.

I finally went into the house and started by sorting out the rubbish; ground floor first, from the front hall to the kitchen. I opened the cupboard and began pulling out boxes of old shoes, piles of newspaper, magazines and comics. I set the comic books aside to sell as collector's items, put the rest in bags and took them out to the footpath by the entrance. I also took out a broken chair, a suitcase with no wheels, bags full of dishcloths, bags full of bags. I found some tools and a vacuum cleaner that looked like Rosey the robot maid from The Jetsons. I opened it, emptied the bag and plugged it in. It was in perfect working order. I tested the suction on the palm of my hand and started hoovering the doorway. From that moment on, Rosey followed me like a loyal dog into every corner of the house, sucking up the dust, leaving a new era in our wake.

Next to the cupboard was a small bathroom, perfect for when you can't hold it in any longer. I lifted the lid of the toilet. There was so much sediment in the bowl it looked like shit had been smeared up the sides. I opened the valve and waited for the tank to fill, then pulled the chain and watched with joy and relief as the water began to whirl, gurgle and flush away. A decent clean and that would be one basic need covered. I unscrewed the seat and discarded it. It would have to be replaced with a new one.

By the entrance, at the foot of the wall, a pile of boxes and bags was already waiting for the rubbish truck to pass. It would take a serious tip to convince them to take it all. I poured half a bottle of liquid detergent into the toilet bowl and another good slug into the sink, which had those classic rounded screw taps with a circle of pearly glass in the middle of each one, a decoratively printed C on the left and an F on the right. The drainpipe was very old, fused together with dirty lumps of Campeche wax – we might need a new tube entirely, and to replace the damp-eroded plaster. Salty residue bulged in big, cracked, foul-coloured bubbles, like mamey fruit or scorched skin. I threw away the old broom, the disgusting plunger and some old buckets. I vacuumed the floor and continued along the skirting boards to the steps down to the living room. I was exhausted and still hadn't even finished the front hall. I needed a pick-me-up – I needed music. I went into the living room and plugged in the turntable. I looked for an on/off button on the dashboard and pulled the miniature lever. The device came to life with an electric squeal, like Frankenstein's monster returning from the dead. I lifted the lid and fiddled with the buttons until I got the plate to turn. I picked a record at random. The cover showed a white-blonde woman in the foreground, with very red lips and a matching dress that almost blended into the dark red background: Peggy Lee. I didn't know her, but she looked nice. I took the record out of the sleeve, slipped it onto the drive and set it to turn at thirty-three revolutions per minute. I lowered the needle arm into one of the grooves: magic. Swinging my hips to the beat of 'He's a Tramp', like the little tousle-haired grey dog from *The Lady and the Tramp*, I went on into the living room. I'd left a woman's shoe in the middle of the floor: size six heels in beige calfskin leather, with delicate leather stitching. How had I not seen it before?

Around the dining table there were eight oak chairs with flowers carved into the top of the backrests. Their delicate varnish had stood the test of time and absorbed the traces of all the bodies that had ever rested their weight against their benevolent wood. A wax-dampened cotton cloth sufficed to remove the layer of dust and protect their dark warmth. The great rectangle of the table was covered with an organza tablecloth with imitation cross-stitch embroidery. On the tablecloth, instead of serving dishes and plates brimming with food, there was a random assortment of mismatched objects – open boxes full of junk someone might have planned to throw away: a roll of cable, a hammer, a little blue copy of the New Testament, a sock, a handful of wooden clothespins, an empty spray bottle, an adjustable spanner, matches, a seventy-watt incandescent Osram light bulb with a broken coil, three apricot stones, a billiard ball. Other objects must have been left there more deliberately, such as the glass sweet jar containing a variety of small items: coins, drawing pins, keys, clips, hair slides, buttons and sewing pins; or like the brass candelabra and the pressed glass fruit bowl full of fake fruit: a badly painted plastic orange, hollow like a ball; a green apple with visible sprues, a banana, a slice of watermelon and a bunch of rubber grapes that fell off the stem at the slightest touch. The kind of grapes I'd always loved to steal from the fruit bowl in my grandmother's house when I was a child, to suck on until my mouth was dry. A cognac glass stood on the corner, by the head of the table; the liquid had evaporated into an amber treacle, mixed now with dust, looking like a drop of resin filled with microscopic particles of memory. It was strange that it should have been left there for so long, who knows how long, right on the edge, without anyone taking it over to the sink or knocking it off and breaking it as they passed.

The lacquered wooden Bauhaus-style cabinet stood under the window that overlooked the parking space and the wall of the neighbouring building. Its glass doors displayed the silver cutlery, fancy crockery, soup tureens, porcelain dishes, decanters and serving plates. On the left-hand wall hung a large still life, an oil painting showing in *trompe l'oeil* a table replete with food: sliced cheeses, bread, figs, knobbly lemons, segments of mandarin sitting in a bowl of peel, a melon with its infinitely sweet innards dripping out, a whole filleted fish. With a handful of white lines, the painter had deftly depicted a glass jug and the liquid effect of the water, as well as an almost imperceptible sfumato – a wisp of steam coming off the freshly sliced bread. Only a careful eye would discern a fly hovering over the fish's belly; it melded into the dark backdrop. A demijohn, a bunch of crumpled peonies and three dead partridges completed the scene. The curious and very irritating thing was that the frame was wonky, as though someone had knocked into it by accident and left it that way, twenty-five degrees off horizontal to the floor. It looked like the fruit and plates were about to roll out of the painting. Naturally I couldn't resist the temptation to straighten it.

By the kitchen door was a cabinet with bevelled glass doors, crammed with decorations and miniatures. In my grandmother's house, opening the glass cabinet had been strictly forbidden. Only she could decide how to arrange its contents, and which items would join the crowded ranks of family memorabilia. But I knew that the key was hidden on top of the cabinet, behind the cornicing, so when nobody was around I would pull up a chair, then place a stool on top, so I could reach the key and open the door. As a child, I did it out of pure curiosity; my only goal was to inhale that still, imperturbable air, to stick my nose in where I shouldn't, in the most literal of senses. I unrolled the little scroll that had been my parents' wedding invitation; their wine glasses were intact, still wrapped in plastic on their MDF bases. I pretended to drink tea from the porcelain set that nobody ever used and played with the tiny ceramic dolls. Over time, however, the glass cabinet turned into a kind of reproach. I placed the crown of roses that my cousin Sonia had worn at her first communion on my head; my parents were sectarian, so I would never wear one of those. Then there was the diploma that Lidia was given for being on the honour roll, souvenirs from my eight cousins' fifteenth birthday parties and their studio photographs with professional hair and make-up. Meanwhile, I tried to contribute things I'd made myself: a ceramic jug I fired and painted in a workshop at the Casa de la Cultura, a glass swan with its head tilted strangely to the side, a set of miniature screwdrivers that looked like they really worked – I'd given them as a present to my grandmother because I thought they were the loveliest, most amazing thing. My marquetry jewellery box with mother of pearl inlay struggled to compete with Sonia's wedding coins or the little angels made from migajón clay Lidia gave out when her first son was baptised, but the competition would have been slightly less unfair if it hadn't been for my mother's intervention. I knew she was the one who furtively removed my offerings. When I reported the disappearance of one of my first leather-bound, stencil-engraved notebooks, she said that kind of thing didn't go in the glass cabinet; she had given it to Mily, Lidia's second daughter, for her to draw in. The postcard collection that my uncle Luis had sent while on his world travels rounded off the misappropriation of my gifts. The swan had vanished, the jug broke one day when my mum's friends were drinking tea – the same friends who never tired of asking me whether I had a boyfriend, my, my, you *are* taking your time. Eventually, the only thing of mine left in the glass cabinet was a bunch of dry jasmine that my grandmother kept because I'd been named after it, and which suffused everything else with its scent.

The record came to an end. The turntable gave off an electric thrum for a few more seconds, and then that too stopped. I opened the glass door defiantly. I didn't want to imagine the stories and rivalries it contained. I was disappointed by its smell of sour perfume. I'd never know where those tarnished medals, heraldic spoons and lace fans came from, nor the miniature Eiffel tower or the little porcelain Basset Hound with its sad, enormous eyes. Instead, I unsentimentally emptied everything into a box and took it out along with the rest of the rubbish. Such objects are precious only in the memory of their owners, and there was no longer anyone around to remember these trinkets.

My favourite part of the house was a narrow, high-ceilinged room that must have served as a dinette or breakfast nook. I was instantly enamoured: it was a cosy, charming space, a kind of interlude between the clamour of the cooking pots and the solemnity of the porcelain dishware. Its simplicity contrasted with everything else about the house. It was no more than twelve square metres, and yet it maintained the double height of the dining and living rooms, which made it feel like the inside of a periscope. The liquid transparency of the glass blocks flanking the space cast a soft light, pale green glimmers sifting in from the languid leaves outside. In the centre was an austere convent table covered in a plastic tablecloth printed with oranges. At the rear, affixed to the wall, a rustic backless bench where I whiled away the hours reading, working on my thesis and drinking coffee, sheltered from the formality of the austere dining room.

I'd imagine the table heaped with platters, serving bowls and soup tureens before they were paraded out to the dinner guests. On the wall nearest the dining room, there was a Purépecha-style cabinet with turned legs for day-to-day utensils: pitchers, mugs printed with an insurance company logo, chipped plates, motley glasses, old jars of Doña María-brand mole, tankards shaped like barrels of Corona beer.

Wire crates of old milk jugs and returnable soda bottles sat on the ground. A rusty needle strung with pink thread still pierced an edge of the tablecloth.

Sequestered here, I feel a bit like Cinderella. There are no cinders, but this corner of the house feels tall and narrow as a chimney: the sun sketches flame-like forms on the clear glass squares. I wonder if Cinderella ever returned to her quarters, her little place amidst the ashes, after marrying the prince – not to sew gowns for her stepsisters anymore, but for her own daughters. The twins grow quick as beans; their dresses seem to shrink and I have to keep taking down the hems. Soon they won't even want to wear them; they'll protest at the childish flounces and lace. They'll covet new colours, ponder styles, flip through magazines, pay attention to what the other girls are wearing. I know I did. Not at their age, of course, but children grow up much faster nowadays. And as quickly as they grow, I seem to stop; my rhythm slows, my worth declines. I'm getting old. Of course I'm valuable: I'm the mother of two beautiful little girls and the wife of a famous photographer. But if I were left alone, without my coats, without my jewels… I took down the sewing box and came down here. This is as far away as I can get from them without leaving the house. I don't want to hear the hubbub upstairs, the preparations for an evening out. Still, I can't help but imagine what everyone must be doing: the girls, having finished their homework, will be playing house, while Oralia irons Eligio's clothes and polishes his cufflinks. Eligio will be shaving; perhaps he'll already have bathed and applied his cologne. He likes to smarten up for his darlings. As if I didn't know. Oralia bustles in and out, in and out of the kitchen. She comes in with the starch, or to look for a rag or the baking soda, or she asks me for a needle and black thread to adjust his bowtie; it's crooked. Because the dinner is to be held at the home of an ambassador from who knows where and the guests are all diplomats and important people. The invitation said 'Strict Dress Code' in gold-embossed letters on hammered paper, thick and intensely white. It came with two tickets, but Eligio pretended he hadn't seen. When I asked what the ladies were supposed to wear, he said it was a work event, so why would I be going? I told him about the invitations and he flew into a rage at me for nosing around in his letters. Even though the envelope clearly said 'Vargas Fam.', and as far as I know I'm part of the Vargas family, too. Then he said, to appease me: Fine, if you insist, we'll go, but you know I'm going to spend the evening with Chava talking about men's concerns; you'll only get bored and complain you've no one to speak to. And he's right. I can't stand the snotty, pretentious women who attend this type of dinner, who stare at me as if I were a bug, a fly licking the lip of the champagne flute. It's true I don't use flashy words like they do; I'm a village girl, I won't deny it, much as I'd like to; I don't know the names of any writers or artists and I'd rather keep quiet, hanging on my husband's arm, watching him wince with shame on my behalf, letting him drag me around like a sack. Well, it's your fault, I told him in the end, for marrying a woman without status, just say it, because that's what you mean, isn't it? And then he tried to calm me down: Alright, woman, that's enough, the next time there's a party I'll tell you in advance so you can read a couple of magazines and have something to talk about. So you'll have something to talk about, the idiot said. I have plenty to talk about. If it were up to me, I'd never shut up. What I'd give for someone to actually listen to what I have to say, rather than the nonsense spouted by those little lady friends of his. I said: Well, have an absolute ball, and say hello to your friend for me, I hope you have a spectacular time. Eligio looked at me mockingly. When he comes home, if he comes home, he'll probably sleep in the guest bedroom, like every other night. He doesn't need another excuse. All the better; at least that way I'll get a full night's sleep. I wanted to shut myself away to sew, but Oralia was ironing. I grabbed the sewing box and the girls' dresses and stormed downstairs, while he went on calmly about his business, not even deigning to turn around. I can count the number of times Eligio has looked at me, I mean looked me in the eyes, really seen me. Maybe three times at most: when the twins were born, when we went on our honeymoon, and when we first met, when his gaze made me feel exposed, naked. He'd come to Metepec with his teacher and some other men to photo-graph the streets and the people. The Indians cursed them, saying their devices were the devil's playthings. My father, eager to prove himself a modern man, befriended one and asked this newcomer to photograph his family. He even brought him home for lunch. My girl cousins flew into a frenzy, desperate for someone to lend them a dress, a comb, some earrings, slicking each other's hairstyles into place, passing around the rouge, which we pretty much finished off among us. People gamely offered us their things, because even if they themselves weren't to appear in the photographs, at least their shoes would, their cameo, their very own fringed shawl. The hall was emptied of chairs and settees and tables to make room for us all, and we stood ramrod straight in front of the contraption. We had to stay still as marble statues. When I came in, the young man's head was hidden under the skirts of the camera and I was tickled to see nothing but the curve of his bottom. But when he emerged and I got a good look at him, I thought he was the most handsome man I'd ever seen. He held my gaze the entire time it took to take the photograph. I felt my face flame as time slowed to a halt and we became the only two people on earth. When he detonated the flash powder over the camera stand, something exploded inside me, too. Later, during the soirée that followed, I got up the nerve to ask if he wanted to see the ranch and the land around it. We went to the canyon and the river; I showed him the fields of crops, the livestock, the pastures. My mother had Lupita chaperone us, but we packed her off to pick some apricots, and while she was still in the orchard Eligio asked if I wanted to come away with him and live in the city. When he went to formalise things with my father, he brought the family portrait as a gift, set in a pretty frame, with a black mount and red velvet trim. We had a civil ceremony because Eligio isn't a man of faith, which made my mother furious. During our goodbyes, my mother handed me the framed photograph and said, here, you'll need this more than we will. That man is the Devil. He'll see that you forget your God and your home. Maybe once you're lost in that place the portrait will remind you of the good life you threw away. Everything was lovely at first, when he was starting to make a name for himself. We'd travel together, go to parties. He'd ask me to wear traditional dress, to speak a few words in my grandmother's language or recount some ancestral legend. Then all of that indigenous business fell out of fashion, I got pregnant with the twins and he started seeing other women. You can sense these things. It was only natural for Eligio to grow tired of someone like me. He became very reserved about everything related to his work. He'd shut himself away in his darkroom or in the studio with his models. He wouldn't speak to me for days at a time. Unfortunately, I never managed to become a lady of the world, as I'd imagined when I was a girl. I can pretend, dress elegantly, follow the latest styles and make a good impression, but when everyone starts to talk about lofty intellectual things I fall silent, or I'll see if anything needs doing around the table; I gather dishes, fill glasses. It's how I was raised. And it's not that I'm stupid: I've read, I've travelled, my parents sent me to a good school. Deep down, though, I'll always be a simple woman. I can't make myself put on airs, fill my mouth with false flattery or fancy words. Now I'm in a sort of blind spot where no one looks at me at all. I'm here, but I'm invisible. There's no use in getting cross and throwing tantrums; he ignores me no matter what I do. Eligio's place is out there, among the lights and smiles and champagne, and my place is here: Cinderella taking down the hem of her daughters' dresses as they grow and grow and grow.

The pantry faced the breakfast nook, but I didn't go in; as soon as the door creaked open, I was hit by the stench of mouse droppings and pulled it shut again. I headed on to the kitchen, which I found beautiful despite the chaos. It reminded me a bit of my grandmother's kitchen, although I couldn't put my finger on the resemblance. It was enormous. The feet of the wooden table were planted firmly on the chequered tiles. It was taller than a dining room table, and broad, as if designed for kneading bread or making tamales by the dozen. I hoisted myself up to sit crossed-legged on the surface, facing the window. I looked around and it came to me: like my grandmother's kitchen, this one had no counters. The fashion for integrated kitchens pushed all action out towards the perimeter, while this layout concentrates everything into the middle; the hooks and racks hanging from the ceiling take care of storage. It's a matter of habits. You come into one of these kitchens and at first you scan the borders for a place to put your bag, the salad bowl, an empty mug. Then you get used to how all activity converges in a powerful centre, warm and well-lit. I glanced up: I'd have to wash the lamp and hanging rack with pounds of soap to remove the grimy crust dripping from the edges in greasy lumps. The refrigerator must have been as old as the house. The stove, too: its large burners were made to withstand earthenware pots, a pressure cooker or the twenty-litre steamer hung amidst black cobwebs from the iron hooks above.

I tried to picture the kitchen clean and bustling, the soul of every utensil restored: the cross-stitched napkins bright white once more, the wooden spoons faintly singed, the basalt mortar damp, its pestle smooth and glossy from hours of pounding and mashing. I could almost hear the ladle peal against the side of the pewter saucepan, the kettle's shriek, the muffled tss-tss of the tomato-shaped salt-shaker, the jet of water from the tap, the clay dishes scraping against each other. I'd set violets in the cornice of the sink, hang a bamboo wind chime so the breeze could announce itself, install a strawberry-shaped feeder for the hummingbirds that darted at the window, startling the silence with their wingthrum. I wanted to fill the whole house with plants: a bougainvillaea to thread its branches into the terrace pergola on the way up to the attic; impatiens, geraniums, roses, petunias, chrysanthemums, periwinkles and azaleas to populate the balconies. I opened the door and peered into the garden: a wild, untended jungle, with all of nature's magic making its own unfettered way, intertwining itself at will. I circled round the back of the house. The footpath led to a black painted wrought-iron door. I imagined it guarding a windowless room, a blind chamber, not very large, confined between the load-bearing walls of the kitchen, living room and front hall. Best not to even wonder what was inside. We all know what happens in stories to women who open doors that men have forbidden them from opening.

To restore a building, the most important thing is a good builder. Not an architect, not a restorer, not a contractor, not an engineer or a construction company. No. A reliable builder is far more valuable than all of them put together, and I knew the most honest and competent one out there, the one who knew the most about the materials and techniques employed on houses from this period, the one who best understood their structure and their soul. Because houses have souls, not only in a metaphysical sense but also in a structural sense: I mean the middle part of a beam, between the joists, what keeps the columns upright, the beams firmly horizontal; what supports the building's vaulted weight, the empty, habitable space that can weaken with earthquakes or simply the passage of time. At least, that was what Lico told me when I was a child and the house next to the workshop was being constructed; when I'd peer in to ask what they were up to and why. I'd spend hours watching him bend rebar to assemble a cage. He'd place each rod between two parallel bars, insert a galvanised metal tube over the end and use it as a lever to bend the metal as easily as rubber. He'd bend it again, then a third and a fourth time, until he closed the square, later using a piece of wire twisted three times with a binding hook to attach it to the cage. The bow-shaped twist secured each stirrup to the four perpendicular lengths of rebar. This slender prism was to be, you might say, the soul of the column; it would be filled with a mixture of sand, gravel, cement and water, contained within a mould of boards. Nobody made cages and columns like Lico did; there was nobody better suited to restoring the soul of a house.

So I went looking for the most brilliant of ordinary men. I knew how to find him. I went to the part of town where all the skyscrapers are; where exhaustion and greyness reign, that crazy excess of concrete and glass, machines building, machines driving, machines walking, machines operating other machines. I wandered round the looming skeleton frames until the sun was high, leaving little shade or pavement to walk on. There was barely enough room for pedestrians to get past all the rubbish and weeds, and they'd have to clean their shoes in the bathroom when they got to their destination. I waited outside a construction site with barriers flaunting ostentatious adverts: this is your dream, come and make it a reality, spend your life savings, last available apartments, roof garden, spa, swimming pool, CrossFit. They used the phrase 'health club' instead of 'gym'.

At 1pm on the dot the workers began to emerge. Dozens of men and a handful of women spread out on the traffic median, seeking the meagre shade of deliberately pruned-back trees. They sat on the thirsty grass and opened plastic bags of food in their laps. They untied the knots that their mothers, wives, girlfriends or perhaps they themselves had tied early in the morning; they extracted the cold food, rice, stew, beans, and ate it with hot tortillas bought by the half kilo from a street vendor with a cool box. Dust from the construction site had dulled all their clothes to nearly the same colour. They had shoes caked with lime, hands cracked with mortar, phones and rucksacks coated in powder. Temples sweating, they squinted in the glare or fixed their gaze on their food. Their faces were mostly relaxed or smiling at some joke. In their yellow helmets, orange jackets and Hi-Vis belts over their dungarees, they were, ironically, invisible. Those who finished eating first lay down for a snooze in the hollow of a wheelbarrow or a slice of shade, legs crossed, helmets covering their faces and rucksacks under their heads, satisfied, owing nothing to anyone.

I just waited. As homogenous as the gathering was, I knew I could spot Lico in any crowd; after all, he was the most brilliant of ordinary men. He too would see me and know I was looking for him. That's why all I did was wait until the sun had heated up the pavement, until I spotted him in the distance, shimmering in the heat. The bell rang and the men and women got up, gathered their leftovers into bags, put the lids on their Tupperware and zipped up their rucksacks, ready to start the afternoon shift. Lico came over from the end of the street, unhurried and unsurprised, as though I was any other of his workers, as though he didn't know why I was there. He was so small that I didn't realise how close he was until he was right next to me. I had to bend down to greet him. He gave me his broad, good-natured smile. He didn't seem to have aged a single year, his muscles were just as solid, his features exactly as I remembered. We shook hands and I felt his calloused palm, rough as wood, accustomed to making rebellious matter yield to his touch.

I asked after his family. He said that his eldest son, the one my age, had headed north and was doing well. Juan was studying engineering, Martha and Lalita were still helping their mum, Carlos sometimes worked with him, and Irma, though he'd rather she stayed home and studied because she struggled at school. And the little ones were around too, wreaking havoc. I told him in broad terms about the house. I explained what needed repairing, as far as I could see. I took great pains to use his words, his language, though I imagined I sounded ridiculous, going on about RSJs, render and downspouts, about replacing the galvanised sheeting and asbestos with PVC. Suppressing a little smile, Lico listened and nodded. He asked for details without a trace of condescension. In his mind, he built the building I described and cast the spell that would make the restoration possible.

Still, he'd need to see the house for himself so he could take stock, calculate the cost of materials and quote for the labour. He'd come the following Saturday. I knew I could count on him. I remembered once hearing my father say: Lico makes you want to pay him double. It's not easy to find a foreman who arrives on time, works hard and doesn't make off with the materials. He said goodbye and I walked back to where I'd parked the car, confident and relaxed. I felt as though in some way the work was already done, it was just a matter of clearing the way, letting time do its thing. That's how sure I was.

The second bedroom, on the right at the end of the corridor, was like a doll's house. Large yet cosy, furnished in wood, it had a double-height vaulted ceiling and a mahogany spiral staircase up to a mezzanine. It smelled sweet, like wax. It was like sticking your nose inside a sealed tin of crayons. Dust had barely touched the surfaces and the passage of time wouldn't have been noticeable if it weren't for the toys, whose manufacture and material were from a different era, early in the industrial use of polymers. The fur of the plush animals was rough and their insides were bursting out as though they'd been stuffed by a taxidermist. The carpet felt softer than in the first bedroom, probably a double underlay, no doubt designed for hesitant first steps, falls, long hours of play on the floor.

Three windows looked out onto the garden, one below, another above, and a smaller third one at the back of the mezzanine, nestled inside the triangle of the vaulted ceiling; all three had wooden frames, bevelled glass and pink gingham curtains finished with lace fringing, tied back on either side with a ribbon. Under the mezzanine were two parallel tables against the back wall, each with a lamp and chair. A bookshelf by the stairs displayed original editions of the *Struwwelpeter* stories in haphazard order, a copy of *The Thousand and One Nights*, a gap where Perrault's stories ought to be; an abacus with coloured beads, a papier-mâché Lupita doll and a slide viewer. I took the lid off a Coloso shoebox full of postcards and letters: the Twin Towers, the Statue of Liberty, Chinatown, the Golden Gate, Pier 39, skyscrapers, parks with close-cut lawns, a ferry, the Wonder Wheel on Coney Island. / We miss you, Mummy, hope you feel better soon so you can come and see New York. / Today we went to a Chinese restaurant and María felt sick afterwards, no one here cooks as well as you. / Tomorrow is our first day of school, we promise to study hard and be good. We love you.

On the wall by the door were two wardrobes built to house all the dresses surely hanging inside. In the corner, a big, overflowing toy box. Dolls stared into the abyss with huge, clear, still eyes. Some of their eyelids had fallen shut with fatigue, others had only one eye open, a macabre wink made worse by the mottled effect on their ceramic skin.

Between the toybox and the window, on a table made for this purpose, stood the replica of a delicate Victorian house with a brick-coloured façade, dark green roof tiles and white-framed windows. A house within a house within a house. I'd always longed for a doll's house when I was small. I created crude improvisations by taping together cardboard boxes and cutting out windows and doors, but my mother eventually threw them out; she called them clutter. A real doll's house was a rich child's toy. I stuck my giant eye to a window. Light streamed in through the back. On the first floor was a dining room and kitchen, with all their furniture and decorations in place. The father sat at the head of the table, where dinner was served, and a little girl stood on the sofa. There was a dark-skinned woman in the kitchen, leaning over the fake stovetop flames, stirring a pot. It's time to eat, Silvia, call your sister. There was a bottle cap full of tiny shreds of paper from a spiral-bound notebook in the middle of the table, a thimble in the father's hands. Isn't Mummy going to eat with us? Your mum's tired, but she'll be down later, let her sleep, eat up or she'll tell us off. / María, come down, it's lunch time! / When you're finished we can go to the cinema, and if you're good I'll take you for an ice cream, but only if you finish your vegetables. / Come on María, we have to eat our vegetables! Can I have a banana split? Hmm… maybe, if you eat everything, we'll order one for the three of us to share / No, I want one just for me / Don't be silly, sit down and eat, it's getting cold. / María, come down now, we're going out for ice cream! / Aren't you coming down, darling? / Maybe she got stuck like Mummy / Don't say that, eat up and then we can go. Oralia, can you go and find María? Silvia, don't drink so much water, you'll fill up and won't finish your food. Sit down properly. / It all seemed real: miniature lamps hanging from the ceiling, miniature cushions, miniature flowers in the miniature vase. Miniature stairs leading up to the miniature second floor, where there was a bathroom with a bath and a washbasin.

The steps of the spiral staircase creaked under my weight. Had the wood been asleep, or did it always creak when a weight like mine made its way up to the mezzanine? Under that steep, vaulted ceiling, it felt like being in a warm cave, designed for slumber and seclusion. There were two single beds, each with white headboards and bedside tables. The wallpaper, adorned with bunches of roses, matched the quilts. Tucked among the cushions were more dolls and stuffed animals – the favourites. / Choose one. Please, María, you can only take one, you have to understand. Silvia's already got Nona, which one do you want? / No. / Don't cry, please, you can't have Poncho as well. It's Poncho or the doll, you have to choose. / No. / You're only allowed one at boarding school, if you take more they'll be sent to the headmaster. Can you imagine Poncho in the headmaster's office? You're better off leaving him here, he'll be waiting for you with his friends, OK? Don't cry, darling, you'll love the new school. There's Disneyland in the US, that's where Pluto and Goofy live. Leave Poncho here, come on now, let go, let go! That's enough tears, bring your things. Oralia, can you lock up, we're leaving. Oralia…

The sun came in through the window and cast four slats of light on the quilt. I lay my head on a cushion like Snow White when she arrives at the Seven Dwarves' cottage. I hugged Poncho and found myself thinking about the possibility of letting the pregnancy continue its course, letting the cells divide towards their specific functions, letting the organs' membranes knit together until they formed a body. A house within a house within a house. It was a complex, strange decision: I wasn't suddenly overcome with the desire to give birth, turn into someone else; rather, I longed for inaction, dreamed of letting inertia take over, surrendering to its plans. I had a roof over my head, solid walls sheltering the hope of a life together. Of life, full stop – nothing else was necessary.

My hand came across an object hidden under the pillow. It was the other doll, the girl who hadn't wanted to go down to dinner. So far from home, I thought, poor thing. Her hair had been yanked out, her head twisted round, her arms broken, her dress ripped, there were bite marks on her rubber heel and her face had been scribbled on. Her eyes were two black holes where a pen nib had been plunged in hard.

I was in the kitchen, taking another inventory of salvageable pots, utensils and dishes, when the doorbell took me by surprise. It rang twice, three times. I figured it was some salesperson, or perhaps Zuri coming by before his trip to pick something up, to say goodbye. I went to the door, but the blue and red lights stopped me in my tracks. I stepped back and peered out of the living room window. Through the gaps in the fabric, I could make out two police officers on the pavement beside an old lady, as thin and brittle as a dry stick. Climbing onto the back of a sofa for a better look, I lost my balance and had to catch myself against the window. The old woman immediately pointed at the shifting curtain and shrilled, there, I'm telling you, there's someone there. The officers, a man and a woman, hands on their hips, looked at the window. I know the owner, he lives in the US but he hasn't been back for ages, I noticed yesterday that there was someone inside, burglars, or God knows who it could be.

A shock of fear ran through me. I had no way of proving I was there legally, that the heir to the house had asked me to do the restoration – I hadn't processed the documents yet. But even if they assumed I was a squatter, I thought, they probably couldn't arrest me, they couldn't break into the house without a warrant. I clung to this hope as I watched the policewoman open the corner gate. She entered and came up to the window, stood on tiptoes and shielded her eyes to peer through the lace. I got down from the sofa and pressed my back against the wall, my pulse racing as though I was playing hide and seek. Suddenly the turntable let out a crackle, the disk began to spin again and the tonearm moved automatically: *He's a tramp, but I love him...* sounded in the cavernous house, and outside I heard the old woman exclaim, Can't you hear that? That's music, I'm telling you there's someone inside, there's someone in there!

The policewoman followed the footpath around the house, towards the chimney. I saw her shadow pass the French doors, all the way to the dining room. I was paralysed. She shaded her eyes again and brought her face to the glass, only this time I was right there in front of her. She called out, señorita, please open the door. When she saw I wasn't moving, she shouted to her companion and muttered a code into her radio. I took advantage of her distraction to unplug the turntable and dash upstairs. I heard a distant siren getting closer.

I peered out of the Chinese room. Another police car arrived and the male officer approached on the footpath too. They knocked on the door and ordered me to open it. The old woman was staring at the house, her nose scrunched as though she'd caught a whiff of rotten fish; she was ugly and gaunt, dressed all in beige, her slicked-back hair dyed burgundy with stark white roots. They'll leave, I thought. They'll get tired of knocking and they'll leave. But I still hadn't got my breath back when I heard the door opening. I hadn't locked it, all they had to do was turn the handle. I heard them calling from the hallway. I had to find somewhere to hide, but where? Wherever I went I'd be trapped, on the stairs, in the attic, the wardrobe… Then, from the street, I heard a deep, firm voice saying: May I ask what's going on, officer? I looked out of the window but couldn't see who it was; the newcomer was hidden by the foliage. The voice sounded vaguely familiar, though I couldn't put my finger on who it belonged to. Inside, the house was silent again. The officers had returned to the footpath, and I heard them asking, are you responsible for this property? Yes, the newcomer said, how can I help? The old woman whined something; he ignored her and went to talk to the police officers. I could hear murmurs of conversation but the old woman's voice was shrilling over the words. There's someone in the house, son, an intruder, someone, she saw them, ask her, I noticed the other day, there were shadows and a light on, and before that there were people upstairs, too, I saw them…

The two officers who'd come through the gate left, the other two got out of their car and all four of them surrounded the young man who claimed to be responsible for the property. The old woman was trying to butt her way into the circle, peering into windows. They approached the enclosing wall. From this new angle I could see them clearly, although the newcomer's face was obscured by the visor of a cap with a Raiders logo on it: a pirate wearing an eyepatch and two crossed cutlasses behind his head.

In the third bedroom, there was a motionless rocking chair facing the window and a Singer sewing machine on a mahogany table with a cast iron base, a pedal and a wheel, covered with a green towel. A cutting table with two work surfaces piled with rolls of fabric. An armless, legless, headless sewing mannequin mounted on a pole with a round base. A dresser full of sewing paraphernalia: thread, buttons, zips, elastic, threaders, needles, dressmakers' chalk, large and small bias tape makers, pins with flat metal heads, coloured ballpoint pins, hook and eye fasteners, poppers, Velcro, lace, pellon fabric, ribbons in different widths and colours, measuring tapes, balls of wool and bobbins, a lint brush, a pin cushion, a 4mm crochet hook, a stitch ripper, Barrilito scissors, rounded tip scissors, long dressmaking scissors. A wardrobe full of ordinary women's clothing: dressing gowns, pyjamas, cotton t-shirts, hand-knitted jumpers. I sat on the chair in front of the machine. It was a wooden swivel chair with a metal mechanism, one of the first office chairs ever invented; the cushion had been thoroughly flattened by someone's weight over hours of sitting. I thought how much my mother would have liked this room. I looked at the Singer, one of those immortal machines passed down through the generations along with recipes, remedies and sayings, along with household habits and household saints, along with secrets and manners and tones of voice. Machines that dressed the home in tablecloths and curtains, that dressed bodies in something homemade instead of shop bought, that could sort you out in a fix: a napkin, a costume, a fallen hem or tear down the back of a school uniform. Machines that let things out and took things in, that mended things that were broken. I knew the basics; I could use it to sew some new curtains for the house, at least. But that would be going above and beyond the work of restoration.

Next to the Singer was a little bookcase with smooth, locked doors, painted a cherry red that was peeling around the edges to reveal that it had once been grey, and before that pistachio green, and before that, perhaps originally, white.

Gertrudis paged through a fashion magazine in a patch of garden shade as the twins, sitting on a chequered tablecloth, played picnic with the slim, elegant grown-up dolls their father had bought them at Blanco's. Amparito, Oralia's young daughter, was barefoot in the dirt, chasing Trini, the household cat.

The sunlight forced its way through the clouds and the garden seeped a faintly suffocating herbaceous heat that Ger tried to mitigate by taking great gulps of lemonade, crunching the ice between her teeth. Suddenly, as she flipped a page and looked up, she saw him peering through the lattice, crouched behind the parapet. It was Salvador. Chava, Eligio called him. Startled and embarrassed, she pressed a hand to her bosom and wondered how long she'd been unwittingly observed. Had she done anything indiscreet? She thought of the awful flowery cotton dress she was wearing, so plain it could have belonged to one of her cousins from the village. She called out to Oralia in the laundry area and asked her to take the girls for a bath. She approached the wall.

'Oh, this is a surprise! We weren't expecting you

today. Eligio is at the laboratory, would you like me to call him?'

'I need you to help me with something, dear. Do you have a moment?'

'Of course, let me open the gate…'

'Please, no need.' He set one foot on the base of the wall and started to climb.

'My goodness, don't do that, you'll soil your clothes.'

He jumped into the garden and brushed off his cream-coloured trousers.

'It's an emergency, Ger. I don't know what to do, I've got a complete mental block.'

He went to her and planted a kiss on each cheek. She returned his greeting clumsily, not knowing quite where to lean in, her face colliding with his, damp and clean-shaven.

'Are you all right?'

'Yes, but if I don't have a gin in the next two minutes, I'm going to pass out.'

'Please, come in.' She gestured to the kitchen door into the house, feeling dazed by the sun.

'Was that just lemonade you were drinking?'

'Yes, would you like me to pour you some?'

'No, gin. It's all I can drink at a time like this.'

The mosquito screen creaked.

'Eligio might be another half-hour, perhaps more.'

'Forget that useless philistine – he waved a hand in the air –'He can't even say *oui*. It's you I need.'

She took an ice tray out of the freezer and headed for the living room.

'But how could I possibly help, I told you I only know a couple of words…'

She offered him the ice and he set about preparing a Tom Collins from the drinks trolley.

'Here's the thing. I'm writing an essay on onomato-poeias – you know, when a word mimics what it means…

Remember the poem "Une charogne"?'

She shook her head, but he didn't seem to notice.

'Please tell me you have a good dictionary to hand.'

'I don't know if it's good, it's the one I used at school, but I'll show you if you like.'

'You're a lifesaver, *ma chérie*.'

She went upstairs; he followed.

'It's just a school dictionary, I really don't think – '

'It's very simple, the word *puanteur*. What does it sound like to you?'

'I don't know – something terrible?'

'Exactly!' He gestured excitedly. 'A terrible odour! Why didn't I see it until now. You're a genius. *La puanteur était si forte, que sur l'herbe vous crûtes vous évanouir…*'

She opened the bookcase in the sewing room, took out the dictionary, and looked for the word.

'Quite a treasure trove you've got here,' he remarked, pointing to the collection of missals, old books, letters, chocolate boxes, bouquets of dried flowers.

'*Odeur infecte, odeur fétide*,' she read nervously, as if in a rush to settle the matter so they could leave the room.

'It's a harsh *p*-sound, explosive, like a stomach turning, *pwah!* Don't you think?'

She felt her legs weaken as he approached her from behind. Then, abruptly, the sound of footsteps on the stairs.

'That must be Eligio.' She turned towards the door to put some distance between them.

Chava peered out of the room. 'Maestro! How are you?' he called. 'You're working on the pyramid series, aren't you? Ah, that dark beauty…'

He ducked back in abruptly and seized her, violent, pressing the dictionary between their bodies.

'Let me see you.'

'What do you mean?'

'Let me see you. I need to see you. I need to see all of you, I need to. I'll come back tomorrow, when Eligio is out' – and he pulled away, ready to go.

'Here, you may need this later,' she said, holding out the book.

'Ah, *ma beauté*!' He took her hand and placed a delicate kiss on her knuckles. 'Put a little gin in the lemonade next time.'

The man stepped into the Chinese room and followed Eligio up to the attic. She opened the bathroom door and helped Oralia get the girls out of the tub. She happily plunged her hands into the cool water and hugged María, not even minding that her dress got wet.

Bathrooms used to be huge. It's as if there was a period, more or less from the inauguration of the toilet into the 1950s, when most Mexican architects and builders weren't quite sure what to do with the lavatory. Rural customs were still the norm: a far-removed spot for the outhouse, a separate shack for dousing oneself with dried gourds full of water, while basins and washing areas in the middle of the courtyard served the purpose of sinks, covering facial, hand and dental hygiene as well as laundry and even dishes. It isn't surprising, then, that early attempts to combine the functions of the toilet, shower and sink proved erratic and sometimes failed. It wasn't unheard of, for instance, that the builder would think to install the shower opposite the toilet and put the sink outside, at the end of the hall. In rural houses, the evolution was often even slower: the toilet came to replace the outhouse, while an adjacent shack was used for the shower, so as to take advantage of the drainage pipe; both were covered by flimsy curtains that the breeze would blow open from time to time. In old city houses, it was standard practice to designate a spot at some remove for the construction of a room, smaller than a bedroom, larger than a wardrobe, and there arrange the elements at one's convenience or whim. The porcelain furnishings were usually set at a cold, outlandish distance from one another, although this broad scale allowed for the incorporation of other elements into the ensemble: ideally, a bidet or a tub; a linen or medicine cabinet, a laundry hamper, even a washing machine. Such bathrooms have a characteristic earthy, salty, mildewy smell that not even bleach and great splashes of Pinol can remove, a smell that lingers beyond Glade, beyond potpourri, beyond incense. Their everlasting dimness is often palliated with an overhead skylight or a twenty-watt bulb switched on by pulling a metal ball chain.

In this house, the second-floor bathroom was so ample and serene that, far from being limited to the specific requirements of a lavatory, it seemed to play the part of a retreat, a space devoted to performing ablutions, purification rites, delightful communion with water, to relaxing the body amidst salts and intense heat, the embrace of foam, the fragrance of orange blossom, rosemary, lavender; a silent flame and rays of sunlight filtering through the trees outside, whose shadows danced on the frosted glass of an enormous quatrefoil window with pilaster moulding; a cyclops eye staring out onto the street over the entrance, offering glimpses of birds and a breath of wind. The screen door had several broken panes, and the tiled floor was so dirty that the alternating white and turquoise squares blended together beneath a layer of slimy black mud; the walls and ceiling had been painted over with beige varnish, and the dry film now revealed the burgundy tile below, with rounded trimming halfway up the wall. On the shower side, the ceiling was infested with blisters of damp, sickly scabs oozing salty residue, mould, plaster so rotten it turned your stomach. The toilet, in the left corner, and the sink, set into the right-hand wall, showed the least signs of damage, but the bathing area was utterly repulsive. The corroded walls were caving in, the rusty pipes coming out of the walls, the tub was coated in a skin of grime, mixed with hairs and crusts of soap. I used gloves and a large rubbish bag to collect the shampoo bottles and old creams and long-discontinued lotions. Same with the tubes of toothpaste: they're no longer manufactured with aluminium, no longer have little removable caps. No one uses Frescapié or Mercromina or steel razors with replaceable blades.

The next day, I walked towards Mario's truck instead of going into the house. I approached from the passenger side, rested my elbows on the edge of the open window and said hi, you saved me, I don't know what I would've done without your help. He just smiled. Do you have any time today? I asked. Could we take a couple of trips? He nodded, got out of the truck and followed me. We started carrying out boxes and black bags full of the lightest rubbish: papers, food packages, disposable containers, empty bottles. We amassed dozens of lazily classified piles by the entrance to the house. We set aside the objects that Mario would take to the Xochiaca dump, thanks to an acquaintance of his who sold semi-useful junk: cushions, lampshades, fibreboard furniture, mattresses, bedclothes, broken appliances, frames, faux flowers (vases and all), unremarkable decorations, crochet folders, rugs caked with grime.

In a kind of wild purge, we lugged endless bags and boxes of rubbish out onto the footpath. It was as if the house itself were vigorously expelling its excess detritus, emptying itself. The door was a crevice; time gushed out. Objects fashioned by hands and machines, once useful and meaningful, were now reduced to shapeless matter, bound to dissolve slowly in the magma of the landfill. The house is the empty space between the walls and ceiling that shelter its inhabitants from the elements. Now that the void had been restored, the house could finally breathe, expand its walls, let in the light to embrace its new guests.

'What you told the police – is it true?' I asked Mario as we dragged a mouldy mattress down the stairs.

'Every once in a while I stop by to check up on things, pay the utilities, and collect the post, that's all,' he said.

'But are you related to Don Eligio's family?'

He went quiet. He puffed, trying to keep his grip on the unwieldy mass of the mattress.

'My grandmother…' We manoeuvred our cargo around the curve of the landing. 'She worked here all her life.'

'Oh, that must have been the lady from the other day.'

'You saw her?' he asked, surprised. We paused for a moment.

'Yeah, she was sweeping the path down to the garden. Oralia, right?'

'Ah, so she introduced herself.' He smiled privately and glanced down. 'What else did she say?'

'Nothing… She told me where the power switches are.' We tilted the mattress down for the second leg of the descent. 'And there we were battling for no reason with the kerosene lamp on the day we brought Don Eligio's ashes,' I said. Mario looked confused and tripped on a step. The mattress jolted out of my hands and landed at the foot of the stairs, warped, dark with dust. We went down to lift it up and lean it against the wall.

'You didn't know Don Eligio had died?' I asked.

'No, but it makes sense. I knew he was sick…'

'So yeah, that's partly why I was asked to fix up the house. I think his grandson, or grand-nephew rather, wants to hold a funeral ceremony or something like that… By the way, can I ask a favour? I need a property tax receipt and official proof of address to file for the permits. I'm guessing you must know where they are.'

Mario nodded. He seemed pensive, worried. He drew back the door to the library without any trouble, as if he knew all the house's tricks. He knelt, reached a hand under the desk and extracted a key hidden on a little ledge on the inside frame. He opened the left-hand drawer and showed me the documents pertaining to the house, perfectly in order and at the ready in hanging file folders, labelled by year. Also organised by date, and each accompanied by its respective payment receipt, were the electrical, water and property tax bills, all notices and letters unopened. There was also a thicker envelope that contained copies of documents, as well as some originals: the marriage certificate, the twins' birth certificates. Mario handed me the most recent folder.

'Don Eligio would send a monthly wire to cover some of the expenses, although it wasn't always enough. I tried to keep things in order – some months I'd pay one bill, some months another. It seems that he took ill, because he stopped sending money about three years ago. I paid some of the most urgent things myself, thinking they'd pay me back later, but Señora Silvia threatened to sue me for trespassing and I stopped getting involved after that. I wasn't trying to trespass on anything, I'm sure you can see that. I'm only here because of my grandmother, to help her with the commitment she made. That's all. All the utilities have gone unpaid since the lawsuit. Except the electricity bill.' He smiled, as if amused by the irony. 'My grandmother has always insisted on that, that there should always be light.'

'I see. So you never tried to talk with the señora and clear things up?' I asked. 'They should reimburse you for those expenses, plus the time you spent keeping up the house…'

'Don't take this the wrong way, but I'd rather not have anything to do with them. Don Eligio did my family a lot of harm and the señora has given us plenty of trouble, too. If you'll let me give you a word of advice, I think you'd do well to keep them at arm's length. They aren't good people.'

'Well, they're only hiring me to restore the house,' I said, trying to lighten the mood, 'but thanks, I'll keep that in mind. And I really appreciate your help, you know. It can't be easy for you, considering what you just told me.'

'Think nothing of it. Plus, this is unfinished business for me. I want to put it to bed.'

'Of course, I understand…'

I set aside the documents I needed and we continued piling the truck with junk. When Mario took the first trip, I seized my chance to open the drawer again and jot down the important dates. I went upstairs, guiltily shut the door, removed the winter clothing and opened the secret compartment. First I tried Eligio and Gertrudis's wedding date. I split it into two-digit figures to come up with different combinations and carefully slid the dial from number to number. But the handle wouldn't move. Not on the second attempt, the fourth or the fifth, and not with any other important family dates. I put the clothes back in place and kept cleaning, as if the people who'd lived there might show up at any moment to complain. I wondered what kind of damage and trouble they'd caused Mario and his family. It sounded like there was some intrigue, something murky and awful. Every family leaves something murky and awful for the next generation to unveil.

Oralia opened the door, drying her hands on her apron, said good morning and stepped aside for the man in pale slacks and a grey jacket to enter the house. She didn't even need to announce him. If it's Chava, see him in, Don Eligio had told her in the library seconds before, when she went to answer the doorbell. Oralia gestured to the door by the stairs and said the señor was expecting him. The latch of the sliding oak door ceded softly, with a dull, almost imperceptible murmur. He went in and greeted Eligio with effusive warmth. Oralia made as if to climb the stairs, but lingered on the first steps. She pressed her back to the wall and held her breath.

'What do you mean, you're leaving on Friday!' she heard Chava exclaim. 'That's far too soon. We won't even have time to get sloshed before you go.'

'We'll have another chance before long, you'll see. I'll be back often. Besides, now you'll always have a place to stay in Chicago. You and I have got so many unfinished projects. Why don't we do something here when your book comes out?'

'Deal. I'll hold you to that. Well, believe it or not, I'm going to miss you two. How is…?'

'How do you think? Would you like to see her?'

'No, no. If I do, I may never get out.' Both men laughed. 'Christ, I never thought things would get so ugly.'

'Women. What can you do.'

'Will you be taking the girls?'

'Yes, they're going to Hartford, to Trinity Academy. They'll benefit from some real discipline. Just look at us.'

'Right! Discipline like when you used to sell spirits to the second years.' They laughed again.

'Or when you stole the sergeant's magazines.'

'Ha! Or the time you slipped one into the reports and the major pulled it out in front of everyone.'

'That's right! I'd forgotten all about that. God, they were filthy, those rags... Hey, is the native going with you, too?'

'No, dammit. Oralia took her back to her village and she managed to disappear somehow. I told the fool to bring her back, I'll enrol her in school, etcetera. I mean, she's my daughter! It's my right. But not even that was enough to convince the bitch. Can you believe it?'

'Guess you can't have everything, my friend. What would you say about a visit next summer?'

'I'd say that sounds stupendous. The girls will be thrilled. Especially María, you know she thinks she's in love with you...'

'Ah! Marie, *mon amour...*'

The fourth bedroom was full of saints. I opened the door but didn't dare go in. It was dry, hushed and dark inside. A thick curtain covered the window. It smelled of chrysanthemums. The altars stood in the shadows; images, picture cards, figurines of Saint Jude, the Holy Infant of Atocha, the Virgin of Guadalupe, Saint Barbara, Saint Christopher, Saint Anthony, the Virgin of Charity, clay figurines of ancient gods set among votive candles, incense holders, tureens, bunches of herbs and copal. The main altar was laid out on a table against the eastern wall. There was also a large petate mat on the floor, a pallet dented with the shape of the body that had long slept there, a chair with a wicker seat and Doña Oralia's speckled shawl draped over the back. The room looked like it was part of a different house, a different time; as if the very fact of being there transported you to a cabin in the woods, with mountains and fog and woodsmoke all around.

The day we started emptying the rooms of their clutter, I noticed Mario glancing often at the door to this sanctuary, perhaps wondering what my intentions were. I plan on leaving it exactly as it is, I told him, at least as long as I can. He nodded and smiled faintly. I can help you clean if you like, he said. That was how we ended up taking off our shoes, stepping inside and reverently clearing the altars of dead flowers and spent candles. We opened the window, aired out the room, took out the makeshift mattress and laid the petate mat in the sun. Mario cleaned with a powerfully fragrant green liquid he'd brought for this purpose. He dusted the shelves, the moulding, the shadows of the figurines, the lids of the dishes, the floor. In the kitchen, I washed the votive glasses, vases, incense holders and bowls. Finally, we put everything back in its place, brought in fresh flowers, new copal, bunches of pirul and basil and rue and a box of little candles we lit for every image, until they were all burning at once. Mario began to murmur an invocation between his teeth and his nostalgia seemed so vast and so profound that I was moved to leave the room.

To clean the kitchen, we had to remove cooking pots, dishes and appliances, loosen decades of crystallised fat, layers upon layers of dark and tenacious amber, cobwebs, food residue, liquid spilled a long time ago and never cleaned. I spent days spraying the walls, floors and furniture with degreasing agent, baking soda, vinegar, and soap, scraping with a spatula, scrubbing with a brush and steel wool.

Mario was in the saints' room. He'd asked me to let him pray a novena. Every day, before he got down to work, he'd shut himself away for a couple of hours, and the house would sink into a deep, placid silence. I was absorbed in scouring the stove when I was surprised by a new kind of silence: the refrigerator let out a death rattle and stopped its purring, alerting me to the sound for the first time. How long had it been going on? I had tried to move it when I started to clean, but it felt glued to the floor, and the thought of its putrefied contents put me off even trying to open it. I considered asking Mario to take it away, still closed, on one of his trips, and buying another. Although it would be a shame to get rid of it – it had the charm of a museum artefact, perfectly complementing the period style. Its rounded corners evoked the smooth shape of an egg. Maybe it was true, what people said about the appliances of old: that they lasted and lasted because their parts and processes obeyed a simpler logic, more mechanical and steadfast. I placed my hand on the enamelled plate and felt the pulse of electricity. I turned the handle. The spring released a faint groan, the magnets creaked like dried honey and the light inside exposed an unexpected whiteness: immaculate racks and recesses, the compartments empty except for a bottle of milk and a tray with three eggs. It smelled clean and cold. I picked up an egg and cracked it against the edge of the sink. I turned my face, anticipating the stench, but a perfectly transparent white trickled from the fissure, plus a yolk so firm that it didn't break when it fell. It was fresh. In my bafflement, I wondered whether there might be a henhouse in the back of the garden, populated by hens whose clucking I'd missed entirely. Then I grasped the milk bottle and held it up to the light. The liquid looked creamy. I uncapped it and gave the opening a wary sniff: it smelled sweet. I took a sip and the glossy cold filled my throat, hastening the second swig and the third, quenching an urgent thirst, distinct from the thirst for water, a call of the stomach more than the mouth, deeper, more maternal.

I was exhaling the cool pleasure of the drink when a fleeting shadow obstructed the light from the window behind me. I heard voices, footsteps. I returned the bottle to its place and went to the door. It was Zuri. He was with a slim older woman. He tugged at the door to see if it was open. He couldn't see me; it was dark inside. I opened the mosquito screen and undid the latch.

'There you are,' he said, annoyed. 'I called, but you didn't pick up. We couldn't get in, the front door is locked.'

He took in my slovenly state: dishevelled hair, sweaty face, clothes streaked with grime. I was wearing gloves, a headscarf, an apron.

'Who's that?' the woman asked in English.

'The restorer I hired,' he answered.

The woman raised her eyebrows and regarded the messy kitchen with unease. The walls were dripping with a mixture of soap, acid and grime; there was water all over the floor. Zuri didn't even stop to appraise the chaos. He made his way towards the living room and the woman followed.

'Is she trustworthy?'

'Of course she is, I told you about her, remember?'

'I remember. But I would have preferred that no one come into the house.'

The voices drifted up to the second floor. The blood rushed to my feet when I remembered that Mario was in the sanctuary. I followed, prepared for the worst, but they didn't see him. I checked the door was closed and sighed with relief. I heard Zuri and his aunt in the first bedroom. She uttered a number and there was a pause. I snuck back down the stairs and hovered in the front hall until I heard the woman's livid shrieks, wardrobe doors slamming. I bolted back to the kitchen. The woman shot outside, sputtering insults, repeating it's gone, it's gone. I acted as if I hadn't heard a thing, just kept scrubbing the stove. Zuri poked his head in soon after.

'Wow, you've really been at it.' He seemed nervous, suspicious.

'Yeah, you can't imagine how much junk we had to haul out.'

'We?' he echoed tensely.

'I hired a moving van.'

'Ah.' He seemed satisfied by my response.

'I also hired a builder to do some repairs. By the way, I have a few questions, can I show you something?'

'Not right now,' he said. 'You decide, whatever it is. My flight's at five, I just wanted my aunt to see the house. I came to get some cameras. I also wanted to leave you this.' He laid an envelope of money on the table. 'It's not much, but I hope it can help you get started.'

'OK, I'll try to make it last.'

'She's waiting for me,' he said, and jerked a thumb over his shoulder. 'Good luck with the repairs. See you in a few days.'

I nodded unhappily. He turned and left.

I kept scrubbing. When I was completely sure they'd gone, I pulled off my gloves and apron and went upstairs. Doña Oralia's grandson had left and the sanctuary smelled of candles freshly snuffed. In the woman's bedroom, I found papers strewn all over the floor, the winter clothes dumped onto the bed and one of the sliding wardrobe doors derailed. The secret compartment was open, as was the safe, its contents tossed about in rage: old documents, photographs, knick-knacks.

I took the pack of Parisienne cigarettes from the dressing table and went out onto the balcony; it was broad, and a curtain of dried ferns veiled the view of the street. Neglected as it was, it was the perfect spot to think. There was a set of wicker chairs and one rattan peacock chair. The wicker creaked under my weight. Here, I could take in the forest air from the park without sacrificing my privacy. It was like being inside and outside the house at the same time. I lit a cigarette. I didn't want to cry. Better to feel angry than sorry for myself. I channelled my rush of indignation into banishing all hesitancy. The pregnancy couldn't go on, it just couldn't. I had to do something. I couldn't stop loving Zuri, but I could halt the consequences of my wrong-headed, obviously unrequited longing. The cigarette tasted bitter. I smoked it anyway, until it was spent.

He would come without warning. He'd show up whenever I least expected and shove me into the nearest corner, where we'd kiss and he'd go down on me or I on him, standing up, leaning against the wall. Once we were in the kitchen and I heard Oralia coming. We hid in the pantry and I locked the door from the inside. It was perhaps the most pleasure I've ever experienced. Surrounded by all those smells, his smell, the dark, the heat of the food in their containers. He pulled out his member, I knelt before him and took him in my mouth, softly first, probing his hardness with my tongue and damp lips. I hated doing it to Eligio, but it was different with him; his scent drove me wild and I wanted to swallow more, lick more, draw him all the way into my throat and quell my reflex so I could savour him wholly. He too licked me from in front and from behind, and then I got up and leant my buttocks on the edge of a shelf. Playful, he slipped his fingers into me everywhere, and I was startled to feel such wetness, such desire in me, surrendering with all my bones and flesh until I felt I would explode with the thrill of it. When the palpitations grew stronger, he got to his feet, pumped his member in his hand, gripped my neck and penetrated me. At first I felt only shock and pressure on my throat, which tightened as he thrust harder and harder, until I could no longer breathe and the shelves nearly came crashing down on us. I thought I was going to die. He sensed my desperation, but he wouldn't let me go. When he finally did, I said: I can't take it anymore. Then he bound my wrists with twine, hung me from the hooks where I hang herbs to dry, and took me from behind. I was ashamed of the smell and the mess I'd make, but he didn't care, I think he even enjoyed it. His member was even stronger, even firmer than the other times. When he finished, he stepped away from me without a word, kicked my clothes into a corner and went out. He left the door ajar with me strung up inside, naked, knowing someone could come in at any moment. I wanted to scream, cry out to him, but I just wept in silence, defeated by abandonment and shame. I don't know how much time went by. I was on the verge of fainting when I heard someone opening the door. It was him. He smelled of gin. He kissed me again, crooned to me sweetly, as if I were his bitch and he'd left me tethered in the yard, dying of thirst. He untied me and kissed me tenderly once more. He handed me my clothes and said that Eligio was home, they were off to the club together. I dressed and tried to smooth the creases from my linen skirt. When I emerged, Oralia was charring chiles on the stove. I told her I didn't feel well, I was going to take a nap, that she should please pick up the girls when she was done and I'd stuff the chiles myself. I went up to the bathroom and looked at myself in the mirror: my hair was littered with rue twigs and tansy petals, and the merest whiff of them sent me into spasm.

I made myself a nest in the loft in the girls' room. I took out the nightstand and pushed the two child-sized beds together to make a single broad, soft surface. I cleared the dolls, cushions and quilts, vacuumed the cracks between the floorboards and the mattresses, removing the plastic sheet that had protected them from mould. I covered the bed with a cotton dustsheet, spread out my sleeping bag, clean sheets, my own pillow and the soft blanket I used to keep my legs warm when I was reading. I'd found a canopy-shaped mosquito net in the wardrobe, which I washed and laid out to dry in the sun, then hung from the ceiling of the loft and let it drape around the nest for protection from mosquitoes and other bugs.

That evening, I stopped by my apartment for a shower, something to eat and provisions: torch, water bottle, charger, books, pyjamas, toothbrush. It was to be my first night at the house, and I was excited, like when I was allowed to sleep over at one of my cousins' as a child, thrilled by the novelty, the foreignness of a world governed by other codes and habits. I expected to be afraid, but I fell asleep right away. Maybe it was being up high that made me feel safe, sheltered from any danger or nightmare. I remember I had the most soothing dream. A profound sense of harmony blanketed everything in a peaceful golden light: I was planting an avocado tree in the exact midpoint of the garden. The tree spread its branches, sprouted leaves and yielded round and heavy avocados, their taste exquisite. I cut one down and split it with my hands, revealing buttery golden flesh, so delicious I felt elated.

I woke with the very first rays of sun. My bones were stiff with fatigue from all the days of continuous work. I went downstairs to the bathroom and returned to the nest, ready to relish another spell of sleep. But I couldn't doze off again. I heard the sounds of the house for the first time: the pipes gurgling, the windows creaking in the heat of the sun, a distant drip-dripping, sparrows chirping, a grackle cawing, the clanging bell of the rubbish truck, cars far off and planes close by, the repetitive recording of the scrap metal truck: we buy mattresses, tanks, refrigerators, stoves, microwaves, or any scrap metal you-have-for-saaaaale. I'd brought two books, one by Austen and one by Paz: The day opens its eyes and steps into / an early spring. / Whatever my hands touch, flies away. / The world is full of birds.

The buzzer rang. I wasn't expecting Lico so soon. I rushed downstairs, peered out the window and saw him at the gate with three children, the youngest ones. The whole family was so small. I let them in, sleepy-eyed and apologetic. They must have been up before dawn to drink their coffee, make breakfast, get the kids ready and embark on the long ride here.

'There's no school today, so I brought them along', he said, ruffling one of the boys' hair.

'That's great. They can play wherever they like.'

'All right, you know the drill', he told them: 'don't cause any trouble.'

The kids laughed without a trace of malice, their temperament cheerful and light. Lico shooed them off and they darted into the garden, shouting 'Jungle!', giggling away.

'Here, I'll show you…'

We toured the house, examining every room, every tap, every pipe, every bit of wiring. I did the talking, while he kept silent, nodded, drew closer, sniffed, probed, scratched, took off his cap and put it back on.

'What do you think?' I asked, and went quiet, waiting for his answer.

'It's alright', he said. 'There's lots to be done, but it's alright. It's intact. It can be saved.'

'I'm worried that the crack in the vaulted ceiling might have weakened the structure.'

'What crack?'

'That one.' I pointed to the corner of the living room ceiling, but the line looked solid and even. At most, the layer of paint applied to cover the scar was chipped.

'I'll take a look from the outside when I go up to do the waterproofing, but it doesn't look like a problem to me.'

The shells of olive green paint had peeled outward, flaking off. The walls, previously plagued with salt residue, had healed under the dry dermis and were almost ready to shed their skin.

I explained to Lico that I didn't intend to remodel the house, didn't want to restore it with new materials, like when an old building is transformed into a hotel, the original tiles chipped at and covered over with pathetic imitations of stone, clay or marble. I didn't want to replace the bathroom fittings, the light fixtures, the locks, the metalwork or the taps. I wanted to retain the finishes, restore them as much as possible, remove rust and sediment, lubricate, clean and polish. We both knew that this measure wouldn't spare us much. On the contrary, the effort would be even greater: to repair rather than discard and replace in the spirit of honouring the house's authenticity. It would take more work and probably more money, but it would be worth it. I knew Lico would understand and agree; I could relax on that front. I heard the rumble of Mario's truck and instructed Lico to follow him and pick up the supplies we'd need to get started. When Mario came in, I gave him the envelope of money and let them go, let them take care of the rest. I ran into the garden after the kids, shouting 'Jungle!'

Restoration is a labour of listening. It means standing in the space, or facing an object, pricking your ears and waiting for the silence to conjure an image of what it would look like undamaged. At once, the possible present: how damage and wear-and-tear can add to its beauty. It's a question of hearing the music of time in matter and understanding how objects wish to be restored, what they want to do with that time: conceal flaws and recover sheen and colours? proudly flaunt their deterioration, show off scars earned in the scuffles of time? free themselves of their patina and let their holes breathe, fill the cracks? or perhaps, in a far more dignified way, allow their opacity to deepen their beauty and seek shelter in its weight? Of course, however romantic it may sound to lean in and listen to the materials, you also have to listen to your client and heed their whims – sometimes with tonnes of plaster, acrylic paint and faux gold leaf. I was happy with the house because, as far as I knew, I could do whatever I wanted, restore it to functionality without glitter or patches and permit the traces of time to peek through here and there. When done well, restoration means going against the natural progression of chaos and oblivion. It means defying death by acknowledging its course, opening the door and letting it in, inviting it to live with us. Restoration means creating a beautiful ghost.

A mass of bindweed had taken over most of the garden and draped its blanket over the treetops like a Bedouin tent. Sheltered below was a lemon tree, a loquat tree, an avocado tree and a lemon verbena bush. The longest side of the plot bordered a four-storey building, which cast shade onto the house after five, or after four during daylight saving. At the back was a lusciously damp corner that favoured every kind of life. The jasmine plant competed with the ivy, and the trumpet vine defended its smudge of sun. In the middle, the weeds had devoured the vestiges of a wrought-iron table and chairs. The arrowhead leaves offered glimpses of a broken white and orange parasol.

Luckily, the tendrils of these plants were weak, and it wasn't hard to uproot the invaders. I gathered up the blanket of bindweed smothering what had been deliberately planted there. I used secateurs to trim the ivy, the trumpet vine and the jasmine. I pulled off the dry wild marigold vines that covered most of the façade and considered planting a new one, once I'd whitewashed the walls and cleaned the cantera stone mouldings on the building.

Doña Oralia arrived mid-morning and started clearing the soil for a new vegetable patch right by the kitchen.

She'd brought a basket of seedlings from her own nursery: rosemary, basil, rue, lavender, oregano, tarragon. She was still strong, but she struggled to kneel and dig the furrow. Can I help? I asked. No, child, don't you worry, she said. I have to plant these myself so they get to know my hands and recognise me when I come back to cut them. I kept loosening the earth, pulling weeds and thistles. I returned later: Doña Oralia, I asked, could you help me find an avocado tree? She looked at me with a tender smile, as if she'd divined my dream, and said: I'll bring you one. The best ones grow in my village. She went on working the soil, and then retreated into the house once she was done. As unpredictable as they were, her visits were a comfort to me. Her presence deepened the significance of what Mario and Lico and I were trying to do for the house.

I went out to where Lico's kids were playing: on their knees, faces close to the earth as if bowing down to it or murmuring a secret. The sun lit their heads, glinting iridescent off their straight black hair. They were using mud to make little bricks, round cakes, flower soup, dirt tacos in hoja santa tortillas. How much for a taco, Miss Taco Lady? Some are six pesos, some are eight. I'll have one for six. I paid with a round, smooth rock. The girl giggled and went on tossing her salad of petals and leaves. Sitting on the ground with the kids, I glimpsed a pile of what looked like mud bricks deep in the weeds. I made my way over, pushing through the vines, darting between the bushes. I gasped, my eyes widening. Kids, come and see! I called. Under the ivy was a small adobe structure with an arched entrance; a tiny door, barely large enough for a single crouching person to pass through; and in the entrance, on a bed of leaves, were three little balls of mewling black, brown and yellow fluff, curled against the belly of a tabby cat with eyes like bright gold coins.

The tall windows in the lounge, running alongside the chimney shaft, were made of shell-glass panes. One was broken. Taking advantage of the fact that Lico had the aluminium ladder out, I asked him to remove the pane so I could take a sample to the glazier, because I'd already had the experience of asking for 'shell-glass' in the past, only to be presented with heinous ocean-themed designs bearing seaweed and starfish. I had to explain: the kind of glass used in old houses, with the texture of pebbles or a tortoise's shell. And in the end, I was always told that they didn't have any, or that that kind of glass had been discontinued. I wanted to try my luck in a couple of shops in the Del Valle neighbourhood that serviced houses of the same period with the same kind of windows.

Glass in hand, I was walking along the edge of the park towards Avenida Insurgentes when I saw a girl with very dark curly hair emerge from Café Village: Linda Makina. She was wearing a green bomber jacket with a missing button on the left pocket. She passed me without a glance. I found myself trailing her, my footsteps carrying me of their own accord. I would have rather not known at all, not gone out that morning, not noticed. I would

169

have rather carried on as if I hadn't seen a thing and crossed Avenida Insurgentes in search of the glazier or gone back to the house. Instead, my footsteps ceased to be my own and my heart sank deep into a well. A blind heart that strained away from me like a desperate dog. Linda stopped at the entrance of an apartment building on Calle Boston. I paused a few metres ahead and waited for one of the residents to come out so I could slip in. I checked the names on the letters, on catalogues of forgotten sale items on a shelf. There was a Linda María Robles in 602. I was terrified, but my footsteps led me on. What exactly was I going to do? Tell her off? For what? Confirm my suspicions, or apologise for suspecting in vain? Prove myself to be the idiot who'd let jealousy consume her? Stupid, I was so unbelievably stupid for being there, leaning against the wall by the door.

I heard them laughing. It was them. Their sneering tone was so genuine that I was convinced they were watching me. There were no cameras or windows looking onto the stairwell, but I was certain they knew I was there. Maybe she'd realised I was following her, that I'd entered the building, and now they were howling with laughter at how ridiculous I was. I heard bare feet approaching, saw a shadow cutting into the light under the door. I heard the dull impact of a body pressing against the door to fix its eye to the peephole. I shrank back against the wall as far as I could and climbed two steps up towards the next floor, ready to flee. I was sure they'd fling open the door at any moment to complete the cruel joke and mock me to my face. But the shadow retreated and the footsteps skidded away. On the floor beside my feet there were three drops of blood. I opened my tense hand and yanked out the glass embedded in my palm. I rushed downstairs, dizzy, beside myself, and out of the building. My legs led me back to the house. I washed my wound and tried to calm down. It was just a suspicion. Nothing more ordinary than a green bomber jacket. How could I have let myself do something so unhinged, I was lucky the intern hadn't seen me. I wrapped my hand in a paper towel and secured it with masking tape. Lico was still up on the ladder, scraping the upper part of the walls and ceiling. The flakes fluttered slowly onto the furniture and floor: a snowy landscape. I asked him to return the broken pane to the window. Better for things to stay the way they were.

I called the fifth bedroom the Chinese room. The furniture set was adorned with two parallel gold lines engraved in the smooth shine of the lacquer along the edges of the headboard, the contours of the wardrobe and the surfaces of the twin nightstands on either side of the bed. With every turn, they criss-crossed into a tangle, a kind of symmetrical, angular knot that mirrored its course, in such a way that the lines continued in parallel along the new border until they enclosed an infinite perimeter. I called this motif Chinese without entirely knowing why. Maybe I'd seen it once on the panels of a folding screen or in the latticed partition of a Chinese restaurant. Or maybe I'd read it somewhere. One thing was for sure: I had no idea if this decorative element had any connection to Chinese iconography, or if it harked back to any particular dynasty. Applied as it was to a design as thoroughly Western as a four-piece bedroom, it was probably a period fad in the fifties or sixties, say, that some Mexican furniture maker had used to grant the ensemble a clumsy air of exotic luxury. I bet the catalogue named it something like Black China Imperial Queen, which involved a bed and headboard, two nightstands, a wardrobe and a dressing table with three middle drawers and a cabinet door on each side. In the centre of each door was a circular seal, likewise sketched in golden threads – a symbol of good luck in which the lines formed a labyrinth, also angular and symmetrical, that closed around it. Austerity reigned in this room, an almost monastic, even wretched pragmatism. There was clutter and grime, although the accumulation hadn't invaded every corner as it had in the rest of the house. The objects arranged on top of the furniture were the personal effects of a man past his prime. A solitary man. Objects like a pot of Wildroot cream, a plastic comb, a bar of Old Spice deodorant with an antiquated logo, a bottle of Sanborns own-brand orange blossom cologne, nail clippers. It was evident that this frugal old fellow had adhered in this room to the most strictly necessary aspects of comfort and personal care. The mattress had been spread with a San Marcos blanket, printed with a galloping black horse against a navy blue background, and a lacklustre bedspread I had used to wrap the canopic vase. Now all that was left were languid cushions with greasy shadows crushed into them where someone once rested his head. At the foot of the bed was a very dirty rug, and next to the bedside table, on the floor, a yellow container of O-Dolex-brand foot talcum powder. One of the closet doors was open: three shirts, two pairs of trousers, hangers with nothing on them; below, brown plastic flip-flops that imitated braided leather and a pair of Hush Puppies. The tail of an undershirt peeked out from one of the three drawers. I sighed, weary. There was nothing worth saving in this room; it would be a headache to take it all apart, haul the furniture downstairs, get rid of it. That said, the bedroom could become a comfortable midpoint between the house and the attic, an extension of the terrace: sheltered from the elements, but open to the cool air of the mallows and freshly watered earth. The bougainvillaea filling the trellis would rain down its flowers, scatter them inside. I'd put a Bauhaus armchair in the middle, a few books, a floor lamp with a long arm and half-dome shade that would cast a gentle light onto the chair and nothing else. I knelt before the dressing table and opened one of the little doors with circular seals. That's where I found the black briefcase full of surgical implements. Steel tools sullied with excrescences, carefully wrapped in linen cloths and gauze.

This time, there are several pieces to the costume: a grey woollen cap, an apron with a square neckline, cuffs above the elbow, a long taffeta skirt, white stockings and white moccasins. I emerge from behind the folding screen, not expecting you to be looking at me, and come face to face with your stupefied gaze. I'm unrecognisable. You quietly collect yourself, then ask me to take my place onstage. You've arranged the backdrop while I was getting dressed: a black cloth showing the white outline of a door, hung between two posts, a chair and the marble-topped dresser bearing the set of surgical instruments. The floor is scattered with old newspapers; the yellow fade betrays their age and the open pages show one alarming photograph after another, the headline font and layout very different to today's style. I sit in the chair with my hands in my lap. This time I don't need to do anything, act out a role or adopt a pose. I just have to sit there, at the end of the corridor, as though I'm waiting for someone. I'm supposed to stay still, looking straight ahead, as if you're taking my portrait, a passport photo. You redirect the light from the lamps and arrange the umbrellas to soften the flash. The wings of the cap are making me hot. There are four lamps and the bulbs are very bright. You prepare the oldest camera, the one that resembles a guillotine. Between the structure of poles and rungs, the bellows lies like the folds of a nobleman's neck: the lens looks out of its convex cornea, like a cross-section of a spine. You focus it and cover the lens before slotting the plate into the groove. The sharp blade falls. The nitrate plate isn't particularly sensitive, and I'm supposed to sit still for a few seconds so you can get the effect you want – so you can capture the ghost and her halo, as you explained while I got changed behind the screen. I turn to my left and find the black leather suitcase open at the foot of the dresser, as though someone just happened to leave it there. On the dresser is the tray of tools, the macabre gleam of their blades and tips, their ripping, stabbing, slicing indifference. You've arranged them very precisely in size order, from smallest to largest, and classified them according to specific functions inferred from their ergonomics. The most sinister are the ones without an obvious purpose: which bit goes where, where to sink it in, how and to what end. Some cut, some stab, some extract, some obstruct, some drain, some saw, some separate one piece of flesh from another: pieces that belong to a body, connected to a mind by means of a nervous system, fed by a circulatory system, drained by a lymphatic system, all united under a single name in possession of a consciousness and a voice. I shiver and shake my head to clear it. You glance at me and frown. Maybe you think I won't be able to sit still for long enough for the picture you want. Maybe your mood is darkening because you've realised it's all really happening, the ceremony is real, the beings you summoned are showing themselves, and this fills you with fear. I'm scared too, petrified. Just as you give the hand signal and expose the lens to take the photo, in that very instant, I feel the shadow of her memory in my body and I'm paralysed by fear. The image of a beach flashes into my mind, rough seas, a woman in mourning dress who looks at me as we pass one another. The character *liu* and the photo of the torture victim. It's her, the woman I am right now, in this nurse's uniform, sitting in this chair, waiting for... Keep still, don't move, you say, and I go white, I want to leave, I want to run, but I'm not me anymore, neither my legs nor the rest of my body will obey me. The character possesses me and forces me to stay where I am, fixed before the camera. I'm the woman dressed as a nurse to depict the gross artifice of someone who takes pleasure in hurting others, the very picture of self-sacrifice, assuming the role of the woman who submits her body to torture, her heart to oblivion. I feel sorry for her, for the stupid, incongruous farce she performs when she surrenders to you, dead, as though reduced to something soft and malleable, breaking in the hands of her destroyer. I feel sorry for her, because she is also me.

Come, darling, let me touch you, let my hand caress your bosom, my tongue tease your hard nipples. Go limp in my arms. Come, lift up your skirt, pull down your tights, I won't tear them today, I promise. Come here. Let me drink in the scent of your mouth, your neck. Let me nibble the cartilage in your ear, delicate as a slice of apple. Feel the weight of me, my edifice. Touch it. See how big it is? See what you do to me? Here, let me put it inside you. Turn around. Open yourself to me, like a fruit so ripe you can split it with your fingers. Let me break you. Move your hips, slowly. I'm going to squeeze your neck, but don't worry, I won't kill you, I just want you to enjoy this little death as much as I do. Feel how your hollowness strangles me. No, don't moan. You mustn't let out even the slightest gasp or they'll hear us downstairs and then what will the guests and your idiot husband say? I'm going to pinch your nipples, stiff as the handles of an antique dresser full of secrets, and you'll have to keep quiet, I'm going to enter you from behind and you'll have to smother your shriek, otherwise think of their faces. Say you're my bitch. Bark. Go on, hold onto the railing and bark. I want you to bark like a proper bitch. Bark or I'll stop, I'll pull out and leave you trembling and hot like the hungry bitch you are. You like that, don't you? I can feel you squeeze when you bark. Louder now, so they hear you downstairs, so they think there's a desperate, hysterical dog outside whose owner is beating her, holding her by the scruff of the neck as she struggles to get free. That's it, good. Loudly, louder. So they can hear you, so everyone can hear that you're my bitch. Bark, bark, bark down there too, until I come and my warm saliva runs from your jaws.

From the roof, where he was installing the new tank, Lico asked me to check the water pressure. I turned on the tap in the second-floor bathroom sink. The water flowed fast and clear, but it didn't drain. Lico would take charge of cleaning the sediment, but I didn't want to sit there twiddling my thumbs, now that I'd seen how slowly the puddle in the sink was trickling down the drainpipe without so much as a gurgle. I've always considered the use of hydrochloric acid a mediocre remedy, a recourse for lazy plumbers and people who don't like to get their hands dirty. The first thing to do was to change the P-trap. I put a bucket underneath it, unscrewed the pipe from the bottom of the sink and pulled the tube away from the wall. As predicted, the piece was thick with layers of mouldy slime mixed with decades' worth of grime and hair. I fit the new, clean piece together once I'd covered the threaded end with sealing tape. I turned on the tap again, but the water pooled back into the sink once the tube had filled. The obstruction was further down. I took the P-trap off once more, pulled on some gloves and stuck my fingers into the pipe. I scraped at the build-up on the walls and tugged out a rank, stinking black clump. The whole pipe was full of stagnant water. It was one of those times when you've started something you have to finish, something almost personal, a kind of challenge representing something else: my ability to bring the spirit of the house back to life and thereby earn the right to inhabit it. Then I remembered having seen a drain clearing coil in the laundry area outside, underneath the sink. I went to get it. I inserted the end into the mouth of the pipe and started turning the handle so the spiral would pick up any blockages. It felt like a medical procedure. The coil advanced about a metre and a half, and when I pulled it out a new tide of stinking dirt poured into the bucket, black as squid's ink. The smell was unbearable. I fought the urge to retch. But by then I was far enough into the task that I didn't want to leave the job half done or interrupt Lico to help me with something so trivial. I inserted the drain clearing coil again. As the end felt its way along, I could sense what it encountered: a bend in the tube, a clump of hair. I pulled out the coil and removed the filth again, yanking the clots and clumps from the walls of the pipe, then stuck it in even deeper. It was like having a periscopic eye that helped me imagine the empty spaces in that remote, secret part of the house. The coil got past a blockage that seemed larger and more resistant than previous ones, then reached a wider bend where it could manoeuvre more easily. I assumed it had reached the downpipe. I gave the handle a couple of turns, then pulled. My hands stung inside my gloves. I couldn't scratch my forehead, which was drenched in sweat. The bends I'd navigated earlier were now obstructing the piston's exit. The coil trawled up bits that fell into the bucket along with a dense trickle of ink. The stench was so foul my eyes began to water. I continued pulling out the drain clearing coil until, finally, a clump of slime emerged, which I had to untangle from the corkscrew with my gloved hands. It must have weighed almost a kilo. Inside, drowned amidst its dark tentacles, was the round yellow gleam of a wedding ring.

The cockroaches I'd seen peeping out of the drains made me feel sick, and the hypothetical existence of bedbugs had made me strip the entire house of soft furnishings: curtains, rugs, bedclothes, mattresses, upholstery, tablecloths – Mario took everything to the dump. However, the one infestation that drove me into a panic was the rats in the pantry. Despite all the measures I'd taken to isolate the mezzanine, my dreams were plagued with imagined itching and I'd wake terrified to put my feet down on the floor. The house had roused from its slumber and seemed to be stretching, breathing to a different rhythm. The pipes were regurgitating odours; the wood creaked as it swelled in the midday heat and shrank with the cold overnight. If it had been quiet enough, I would have been able to hear hundreds of little feet scratching away at gaps and depths with their velcro paws.

At first I thought shutting the pantry door would be enough to keep the rats confined to that area, but then I saw a couple slip confidently in through an air vent like they were made of liquid. Naively, I draped a dishcloth over the opening and weighed it down with stones. The next morning the stones were scattered. It would seem my efforts had only made them bolder, more determined to invade. I had nightmares about a murky grey sea full of teeth and squeaks that roiled around me, dragging me down. I needed to use the kitchen. It was absurd to put off cleaning the pantry any longer, but first I had to evict its tenants.

As far as I was concerned, poison was never an option, and it didn't even occur to me to use glue or spring traps either. After all, the house was their habitat, which had been conquered by a colony of mammals – animals, just like me – with as much right to life as any other, even if they were carriers of rabies, bacterial disease, fleas, faeces and filth. Besides, what would I have done afterwards? Kill them with my bare hands? Bury the bodies in the garden? At first, I hardly noticed them, but after a while they seemed to be watching me from the shadows. They'd realised I was alone, that I wouldn't be chasing after them with a broom, and they grew bolder still. They challenged me. They wandered unabashed, not even along the walls but right through the middle of rooms, slowly and cheerfully, scampering up onto the furniture to rub their faces with their little hands and sniff the breeze.

Determined to tackle the problem, I called a number printed on a flyer, one of many dumped on the front step. I asked the woman who picked up if there was any way to deal with the infestation that was less cruel than extermination. 'Of course, we'll take care of everything, don't worry,' she said in a smooth, reassuring voice. We agreed on a time. The next day, a van with a logo of a mouse behind a red stop sign pulled up outside the house. Miriam the pest control woman was around fifty, wearing green military dungarees with external pockets and a heavy lifting strap that accentuated her curves. Her completely white hair was done up like Marilyn Monroe.

When she greeted me, I recognised her voice from the phone, soft as the velvety skin on her cheeks. I held out my hand and she gave me a compassionate look. 'So tell me, how can I help?' she asked, as though the problem was inside me rather than the walls of the house.

I invited her in and she poked around while I described the infestations. She explained her method of controlling and relocating harmful fauna. Do you know the story of the Pied Piper of Hamelin? I nodded. Well, it's very similar. For larger pests, I'll use a low frequency ultrasound device that disorients and attracts them. That will let me trap and then free them in the countryside. For insects, the best method is to use an insecticide that's not toxic for humans and larger animals but perfectly effective for any creature with more than three pairs of legs. The absence of carpets and rugs meant we could be sure there weren't any eggs. We had to shut the doors and windows, fumigate the inside of the house and then wait four hours, after which Miriam would go in and hoover up the remains. Finally, she'd apply a repellent made from vegetable extracts, which would last for at least eight months.

Together we got the ultrasonic pest repellers and traps out of the car. Miriam scouted out strategic places to install them. They had to be left overnight, so I retreated to my apartment for a couple of days while the house filled with smoke. I was sad to see the sorry state my place was in. The rain had got in through the cardboard stuck over the broken window and the sofa and rug in the living room smelled damp and stuffy. I packed my things into a few boxes and asked Mario to help me with this one last tiny move, definitively severing all ties with the outside world. I posted the key through the letterbox, along with a note for the management, written on the back of the notice letter they'd sent. There were only a few days left until the contract was up. I left the building laden with bags and got into my car without looking up at my window, where the edge of the curtain had escaped through the open crack as though to wave goodbye.

We still had to spray the repellent. Miriam carried a tank of it on her back like a Ghostbuster, the applicator tube pointed threateningly at the floor, spraying skirting boards, holes, doorways and the external perimeter. When she reached the door of the forbidden room, she realised we'd missed it. I explained that we weren't allowed to open that door for any reason. Couldn't you spray a bit of insecticide through the crack underneath? I asked. It doesn't work like that, she responded; I have to cover all the nooks and crannies, otherwise something could slip away or get trapped. I really can't open it, I explained firmly. I understand, said Miriam, it's just I won't be able to guarantee the house is completely pest free.

Once she'd gone, Mario and I set about emptying the pantry. We took the shelves out into the garden and I washed and let them air dry in the sun. I rescued a few tins with old designs for Picot antacids and English Breakfast tea, some amber coloured glass bottles in different sizes, a bronze pestle and mortar, and six white porcelain jars labelled in fine gold leaf calligraphy: *Mentha piperita*, *Acanthus*, *Cinchona calisaya*. There were three wooden boxes, nailed shut, which we checked in case the rodents had managed to nest inside, but they seemed to be intact. The bottom two boxes each contained twelve shining bottles of Balblair 12 Year Old Scotch whisky, bottled in 1965. The lid of the third box was ajar. Inside there were eleven bottles of Talisker – one missing.

Guilt is a shadow that gnaws at your insides. I wake in the middle of the night and feel it scratching at the edges of my chest, the walls of my stomach, my ribs; it gets into my bones, crawls back and forth, builds black nests to smother me.

He went to France again without telling me. I didn't know; one day I just started noticing he was gone. At breakfast this morning, Eligio was looking through the post when he let out a laugh and cried: Chava, you degenerate! When he turned the postcard over to read the message, I saw an obscene photo of vedettes from the thirties. Their clothing wasn't especially revealing, but their lascivious eyes and mouths were outrageous and repugnant to me. When Eligio went out I retrieved the postcard from his desk so I could read the message: The ladies send their regards! Cheers! Long live vice!

It was then that I realised how wrong I'd been, what a mistake I'd made to get involved with that madman. My life is settled now, I've got my house and my girls to look after. They'll be all grown up before long and there are so many things I want to teach them before they go out into the world. There and then, I decided I'd never again do such a thing. Never again would I risk losing what was important to me in exchange for something so stupid, a moment of passion, a whim I'd soon forget. I'd had my moment, a little breather, and that was fine, I'd let my hair down, as they say, but now I had to get a hold of myself and go back to what truly mattered. I'd say a thousand prayers: Lord, I have been led into temptation, I have lost the path of righteousness, but I do not wish to live in sin any longer. I renounce my sin. I renounce the Devil, I renounce the wickedness that sullies my soul.

I go up to the girls' room and take their measurements. Whenever I make them a new dress I have to measure them again: the distance from waist to knee, the width of their backs, the length of their arms. Perhaps next year their busts will start to grow. María has been gaining too much weight, it must be her age; I'll have to cut down her desserts and sweets. I show them some magazines so they can choose a design they like. I watch them flick through the pages of the women's section, not the children's anymore: they stare in fascination at the models, the make-up, the long legs, the high heels. Silvia says she wants a trouser suit. I say no, my love, why don't you find a dress, something appropriate for your age. My heart squeezes when I see María point to a grey tunic in the maternity section, as though she wants to vanish under a sack of potatoes.

I let them go back to their games and come into the sewing room, but instead of looking for patterns and fabrics I close the door and open my cupboard. There I am. I look at photos from when I was a bright-eyed young girl, I read the letters I wrote home that were returned, the diaries I kept on my travels. I write today's date on one of the leaves of a flower he gave me and I flattened between the pages of a book by Baudelaire; a little French rose he must have cut from some local garden. My *fleur du mal*. Here it must remain.

Thank goodness for clinics with pink upholstered chairs and framed posters with encouraging phrases about the value of being a woman, sterile waiting rooms where qualified staff carry out the procedure without recrimination or judgement, facilities with sanitary measures, cutting-edge technology and ambient music. The receptionist gave me a flyer explaining the different methods and a form to fill out: age, weight, first period, first sexual activity, number of sexual partners, method of contraception, number of children, previous abortions, date of last period: eight weeks ago.

First there was an ultrasound to check how far along I was and how things were progressing. Then a consultation, a box of pills on the desk in front of me, a little plastic cup full of water. I'd been expecting an actual intervention, so this seemed strangely simple, disconcertingly so. I listened to the instructions: Mifepristone now, then misoprostol and painkillers eight hours later, for the discomfort, which might be considerable. I nodded at each directive. I swallowed the mifepristone and put the bag of misoprostol away, along with the leaflets, the prescription for the painkillers, and the mints bearing the clinic logo which I'd taken from a glass bowl. How apt and sweet are the words 'non-invasive method', when you find yourself under threat of invasion. Why wasn't it always like this, why isn't it like this everywhere, knowing that you can sit before a doctor at a desk, receive instructions, pills, a plastic cup, glug it down and come back the day after tomorrow, make sure someone is with you, here are the numbers to call in case of any complications, drink plenty of fluids, use a hot compress, eat well, preferably chicken and vegetable soup. It's that simple. The hard part would be finding a way to forget, or to replace the memory with persuasive sugar-coated versions in which the assault that caused the pregnancy was driven by pleasure, by desire or love, by a misunderstanding – these things happen.

When I left the clinic, I felt like I needed a drink. Just one, I said to myself, though one turned into four. I went to a little bar Zuri and I used to frequent, near his place, and sat on one of the high stools at the counter. I ordered a J&B, because now was not the time to splash out, considering the house-related expenses and the cost of the doctor's appointment. On the stools next to me were two men in their fifties or sixties. They were talking about a woman, mocking her and the ridiculous things she did in the name of love. The one closest to me was speaking while the other laughed through his false teeth. He explained that the woman had written him a goodbye letter, tormented and pitiful, in which she'd borrowed indiscriminately from Baudelaire, clumsily adapting and reconfiguring words from his poems and imagery, betraying their sense. They guffawed. In a voice dripping with scorn, the one telling the story said she'd called him 'my *fleur du mal*' and that the letter said something like: 'I'll have to forget you like you forgot about me, I'll have to bathe in the waters of Lethe, I'll have to wash away your name, scrub it from my soul and then sleep forever...' He interrupted the quotation to say: 'Darling, if it's that bad, I've got a sponge right here.' And they laughed again. His companion wanted to buy me a drink. He cut across the storyteller to ask: What are you having, gorgeous? The next one's on us. I said no, thank you, paid my bill and left, disgusted, their words leaving a bad taste in my mouth. I got back to the house, threw myself down in the nest and fell asleep.

I found out he was back from his trip because yesterday Eligio asked me to make dinner for four. Apparently he'll be bringing someone called Sara. I do miss him, though I think I successfully hid my surprise and the gut-punch of finding out he was with somebody else.

'What do you think about duck confit? Or would you prefer meatloaf?'

'No idea, woman, that's your business. And tell Oralia to take the girls early, they can spend the night with her. We're going to the opera afterwards, *Turandot* is opening tonight. Chava could only get two tickets, but we'll figure something out.'

The food is almost ready when I hear him arriving; as always, far too early. Oralia opens the door and he comes straight into the kitchen. The onion soup is waiting on the stove, ready to be served with the cubes of cheese and bread already arranged beside the bowls. The steamed, julienned vegetables and mashed potato will go with the duck thighs, which are just crisping off in the oven. For dessert I was going to make chocolate cake with blackberry compote, but I decided to do a strudel instead – Eligio prefers it. I even bought a litre of vanilla sorbet.

I meet him in the breakfast room. I try to keep my distance as I greet him, but he seizes me in his arms at once and gives me a passionate kiss that I have to interrupt – I can hear Oralia calling out from the door to say that she's leaving. I go out and say goodbye to the girls. When I return, I see that he's poured himself a glass of cognac. He downs it, refills the glass and leaves it on the edge of the table. He comes over to kiss me again, but I go to the counter and get out the dishes and cutlery as an excuse to avoid him.

'I hear you're bringing your girlfriend,' I say in a voice laced with reproach.

'Not at all, your husband's been exaggerating. Sara is just a friend. What, aren't I allowed to have friends?'

'I never said that.'

'No one could replace you, *ma délicieuse*. Besides, Sara is an idiot who can't even boil an egg.'

'Guess what I've made.'

'Mmm… I can smell something fatty, something sweet…'

'*C'est confit de canard.*'

'Oh! *Mon amour!* What a marvel, come here let me kiss you. You smell like tuberoses; I missed your perfume…'

I let him grab me round the back, sink his nose into the base of my neck. He rests his member against my hip, I can feel him through the fabric, I can't resist. He pushes the chair at the head of the table aside and presses my body against the edge of the table. He lifts my dress and sticks his fingers between my legs, finds me wet and willing. He pushes my legs apart. I say no, I can't.

'Just let me feel you, Ger. I've missed you so much…'

'No, please, I mean it, it could turn into a disaster. And besides, Eligio…' I push his hips aside to try to get him off me.

'I know, *mon amour*, just half a second. Just let me feel you and I'll pull out, I promise.'

He hikes up my skirt and pushes me over, unbuttoning his clothes. Yanks both my wrists behind me. He hauls my arms above my head and I'm at his mercy. What are you doing? I say. Let me go, please! But my complaint only makes him pull harder. It really hurts, it feels like he's going to dislocate my shoulders. He leans his weight over me and crushes my face against the tablecloth. The pattern on the brocade presses into my cheek. He penetrates me, pulling hard on my hair so I can't move my head, and begins to ram into me. I try to tell him to stop, Eligio will be here any second, let me go, I'm in real pain, but he silences me with a tug of my hair and another of my arms as he says: Shh, shh, keep still, you bitch, keep still, that's it, that's how I want you. He rams me even harder. I notice the changing light, the shadow passing by the window. I twist desperately, but he holds me down even harder. I hear the spring of the kitchen door and the mosquito screen knocking three times against the frame, the legs of the chair opposite us being dragged, the camera clicking. He groans in pleasure and as he goes limp he releases my wrists and hair. I lift my head and see Eligio raising his glass in a toast. He drinks and sets it down, empty, right on the edge. They both laugh like little boys who've just pulled a prank. They laugh hard, big belly laughs. I feel him pull out and move away from my body like someone pushing back, satisfied, from a plate scraped clean. He zips up his trousers and tucks his shirt in. I want to say something, to defend myself, fight back, ask questions. But I have no words, only tears. I pull my skirt down to cover my backside. I realise my knees aren't responding and crumple to the ground. I hear their laughter, their insipid conversation. Between the legs of the chairs I see them move away, singing *In questa reggia, or son mill'anni e mille, un grido disperato risonò...*

The nurse smiles at you. She pulls an alluring face and you go over to her, stroke her hair back and graze the fabric of her cap with your hand. The fresh air feels pleasantly cool on my scalp, although the lamps are still on and emitting heat. The nurse undoes her apron and you help her remove it, along with the crisp taffeta skirt. You take your time over the stockings. She spreads her thighs before your face and you blush. She's now wearing nothing but the low-cut cotton tunic, as though getting ready for bed. She shakes her hair down her back, she wants you to look at her, take in the bare skin of her neck and shoulders. I can sense your desire, but you get a hold of yourself, prepare to make the adjustments before the next photograph. She moves into the shadow, lying down on the ottoman with a placid, feline carelessness. She knows her role. She knows what happens next and relishes every instant that leads us towards the conclusion. She knows what to do with the tray on the floor. You had to arrange its contents before the session began, and while you did so, visualising the result, you thought about the title of the photograph: *The Opium Smoker.* Lying on her side, the nurse drops her left hand, her index finger touching the lids of various pots, a bronze one adorned with flour-ishes, another made from white porcelain, another from Murano glass. She studies the long pin with its little soot brush on the end, the deep, rounded spoon with its polished bone handle, a glass lamp full of fuel, a lighter, an old syringe with metal applicator and glass vial, a rubber band. The most important piece in the collection is a long marble pipe with relief carvings: dragons, clouds, bald Chinese men with lascivious gazes. It looks like a flute. The pipe bowl has already been prepared with a measure of 'crow slices'. She pushes herself up onto her right elbow, lights the lamp, returns it to the tray, picks up the pipe, holds the bowl to the flame and takes three deep breaths of acrid smoke. I sink. I focus on the patter of raindrops on the window. The skin of my cheek melts into the ottoman's velvet. My body feels further and further away: my prickling skin, the weight of each muscle, a slight nausea I manage to suppress. She closes my eyes and surrenders to sleep.

Meanwhile, you're moving the lamps and installing the Graflex opposite me. You slip a cushion behind my back. It's a big cushion, I can feel the rough gold tassels pressing into my flesh. You gather the front of the tunic and lift my weight so you can pull it over my languid arms. I know my skin must be cold, but I can't feel it, I just know it, a heavy cold, as though I were sinking into a pool of freezing water. You settle me onto my side. You ball up the tunic and tuck it under me so my pubis faces outwards like in Fortuny's *The Odalisque*. My head tilts upwards. You bend my legs slightly, arrange my feet and hands: my left arm hangs loose beside the tray with the pipe, my right arm rests on the curve of my hip. You place a rough object in my outstretched hand, something with sharp little bumps. An object that feels organic, but dead, dry. Finally, you position something flat and heavy behind me to serve as a backdrop. The smoke weaves through the slats in my mind, bifurcating reality, and I discover I can follow it along one of its branches. The urge to escape my sightless body jolts me awake inside the eye of the Graflex. From there I can see myself naked, lying in the light, a starfish in my hand, the tray with the pipe and pots on the floor, the ottoman, the gold-tasselled cushion. At my back, you've placed that painting of rough seas from the library. I see your pupil through the viewfinder. You adjust the focus. I hear other footsteps. They aren't yours, you're standing behind the Graflex and the steps are advancing slowly from the doorway, treading hard and growing louder. You take the first photo. The shutter closes for an instant, and when it opens again, there he is: the man in a white coat is sitting on the ottoman at my feet. His trembling, desiring hand is millimetres from my skin. He looks at me, drinks in the nurse's drowsiness with his gaze. I want to run. I want to run, but my feet are sinking into quicksand and the sea threatens to swallow me up. I want to run away from here. You take another photo, and just as the shutter opens I feel the touch of his hand on mine.

I buckle the suitcase, put my flat shoes on, pick up my bag, leave the note on Eligio's desk and call a taxi from his telephone. I'm told it'll be a few minutes. I do these things on automatic, without thinking, because otherwise I couldn't bear it. I go into the kitchen and ask Oralia to pick the girls up from school and look after them until their father arrives and gives her new instructions. She gives me a silent, understanding look, then blesses me as though she knows I'm bound for somewhere far away. I wait until she's back in the kitchen before heading out. I put on my gloves, pick up the suitcase I'd hidden behind the door and step into the street. I see the taxi parked on the corner and quickly get into the back seat, my heart racing in case Eligio comes home, in case someone sees me. To the North Bus Terminal, I tell the driver. He sets off without asking whether I'm going to visit family, whether I'm going alone, whether I'm married or have children. Grateful for his silence, I watch the city go by through the window. Everything looks different, somehow, now that I'm free.

I quickly find the Flecha Amarilla ticket booth, the gate, the platform where I wait for a bus that will take me to my hometown. I hand my suitcase to the porter and board the bus. I requested a window seat. I'm nervous. I don't want to have to share a row with some sleazy old man, some nosy señora who needs to know my entire life story. But the bus is half empty and no one sits next to me. I'm excited, like a young girl. Gradually the buildings peel away from the road until they give way to forested countryside. The sun starts to set. The girls will be getting home by now, Eligio will be another couple of hours yet. He'll go into his study and read the note. I feel a stab of vertigo in my stomach like the firing of a cannon, and it's the force that carries me away, at all speed.

When my heart finally stops pounding, I give in to a deep, carefree sleep. I'm exhausted and heavy beyond what my body alone can feel. I sleep, I wake, I look at the landscape through slitted eyelids and sink again, head nodding. I come to when I begin to recognise the light, the shape of the mountains. The landscape and the light reanimate my spirit. I count the years: fifteen. The mere sight of this land is enough to make me feel like an uprooted tree that's been set down again where it belongs.

We enter the town, which is now almost a city. It's changed so much I don't recognise the streets, the businesses, the colours. The bus pulls into a newly constructed terminal. They used to park on the street where the market was and from there it was only three blocks to my mum's house. I get off, disoriented. An old man takes my suitcase and leads me to the taxi rank. I let him. The man asks me to pay him and I hand over a ridiculous sum for the service of carrying my suitcase a hundred metres when I could have done it myself. The taxi driver also charges me an exorbitant price to take me twenty blocks. I'm almost out of money. I'll have to borrow or find a way to earn some; I'll figure something out. Despite this problem and my distress at having left the girls, I feel light as tissue paper. What I need now is to recover away from them; I don't want them to see me like this, to know anything's wrong. I'll have time to think about what to do. I'll send for them as soon as I'm settled in my mum's house.

The taxi pulls into my childhood street and stops outside the house where I grew up. My heart turns to stone: the windows are bricked up, planks of wood are nailed over the gate, the façade is crumbling and weeds are growing among the roof tiles. The driver asks if I'm going to get out. So I do. I wait for him to leave before starting to walk. My aunt Sarita's house is three blocks up the road. I wish the porter from the station were here now to help me carry the suitcase, to get my money's worth. I pass a bakery and buy some pastries so as not to turn up empty handed. That's my last few cents gone.

Aunt Sarita hasn't changed at all. For twenty years, ever since my uncle was killed fighting the Cristeros, she's been wearing the same black blouses buttoned right up to the neck, the same shiny gabardine skirts, her hair tied back and her face sullen. I knew she'd be surprised to see me, but she cried Ave María purísima! and looked at me with a mixture of pity and horror.

'What are you doing here?'

'I've come to visit, auntie.'

'Visit who? There's no one left.'

'Well, to see you, auntie.'

'Don't talk rubbish, girl. Come on, in you come. I'll put some water on for a Nescafé.'

I'd learned of my father's death when my sister Lupita rang to say he'd been attacked, his body riddled with bullets. She asked me not to go to the funeral, so as not to upset my mum even further; besides, how could I think of setting foot in the church or graveyard having sinned the way I had, unmarried as I was in the eyes of God. I'd had to grieve for my father from afar. It was barely a year before my mum caught pneumonia and followed him. The same thing happened: Lupita rang and said it would be better if I stayed in Mexico City to say my prayers from afar, that I ought to worry more about the salvation of my own soul than that of my mother, who had died a saint.

I'd assumed someone had remained in the house, but Sarita said everyone had taken their families and left town. When my mum died, they sold the property and divided up the profits between the brothers, plus one part for the sisters to share. Everyone went their own way.

'So go on then, what brings you back here,' my aunt asks as we're having our coffee at the kitchen table.

'Some awful things happened, auntie. With Eligio. I can't stay with him.'

'Oh boo hoo – don't be such a child.' She let out a derisive little laugh that made my blood boil. 'Things always get messy, but you just have to put up with it. You put up with all of it for the sake of your daughters, so you can give them a respectable home.'

'But auntie, you don't know…'

'Of course I know, you don't need to tell me anything. What, you think I was born yesterday? I know what happened and what's going to happen, but none of that's any excuse for abandoning your husband and daughters.'

'No, I'm not abandoning the girls… I just need to figure out a way of bringing them here.'

'What for? You want to bring them to this infernal place? Their life is there, they need their parents together, can't you see the harm you'll do by bringing them here? And besides, what will you live off?'

'I don't know. I thought I might start a business.'

'By yourself? How do you expect to live by yourself, without a man? You're out of your mind, Gertrudis.'

'With all due respect, auntie, you live by yourself...'

'Exactly, girl, I know what I'm talking about. Now listen up. You can spend a week here and rest as much as you like, but then you're going back. There's nothing for you here.'

To wash surgical steel instruments, you need a multi-enzymatic detergent or pH neutral soap dissolved in demineralised water, roughly 7.5 millilitres per litre. You mustn't use corrosive, abrasive or acidic agents, saline solution or alkaloids. You must use disposable latex gloves to avoid any possible contamination. First you disassemble each instrument; you open the jaws of the haemostatic forceps, pull apart the ratchet, meticulously clean the edges and notches, remove the blade of the scalpel and deposit it in a special receptacle for the disposal of sharp, infectious objects. You must completely submerge the ring handles and shanks, then leave the instrument soaking in the solution for at least twenty minutes before scrubbing it with a nylon brush. Finally, the instruments should be left to dry on a clean towel, preferably cotton, making sure they're laid open and spaced out before proceeding to their sterilisation.

I arrived at my aunt Sara's on Wednesday. That night, in a dusty, stale-smelling room, I slept like I hadn't slept in a very long time. I felt that, by recovering who I had been before I got married, my soul would become a little girl's again: I would be cleansed. I couldn't forget what they'd done to me, but I could pretend it was far away, as though someone else had experienced it. A week is enough to find a way to live here, I thought. I could bake bread in the wood oven at my mum's house and sell it, take out a loan to buy wood, eggs, milk, a sack of flour, a sack of sugar. That was all I needed. On Thursday I went to my mum's house, opened drawers and rekindled my nostalgia. I tried to get the kitchen up and running. On Sunday afternoon Eligio arrived. I heard his voice as I entered my aunt's house, back from the market. The two of them were talking in the living room. Who knows how he figured out where I was. My aunt stood up when she saw me and said, well, I'd better leave you two alone to chat. Come up to my room when you're done, please. Eligio tried to give me a hug, but I brushed him off. Don't be so dramatic, woman. He explained that it had only been a game; an adult game, but a game regardless. When I tried to protest, he insisted I'd been up for it from the start, insinuating he knew everything that had gone on with Chava. It doesn't matter, woman, all couples do these things to stop themselves getting bored – or are you going to tell me you didn't enjoy it? I don't blame you, Ger, we're worldly, open-minded people, we're beyond all that prudery you were taught as a child. Now, if you didn't like it, I respect that, we'll forget all about it and that's that. But enough of your tantrums, the girls need you. He handed me some cards they'd drawn in coloured pencils: a house, a tree, a bird in the sky, *I love you, Mummy*, a red heart, a happy sun.

I went to my aunt's room to tell her I was leaving and to thank her. Shut the door, she said, come here, sit down. Now tell me what you need to tell me. I fell apart, unable to hold it back any longer. Auntie, I don't know what to do, I'm expecting, I said, and began to cry. She was silent, as though she'd known from the beginning. She waited until I calmed down. Everything has a solution, child. You do as your husband says, trust him, obey him, until death do you part. There's nothing worse than solitude for a woman, you hear me? No torture worse than being alone. She gave me a forced hug, stiff as a branch. Then she let me go, jumped to her feet almost happily, and said, now don't you worry! You've got something that will keep him by your side no matter what. She opened the trunk at the foot of the bed, took out a biscuit tin and handed it to me. It was as heavy as a meteorite. It's your part of the sale of the land. Your mother asked me to keep it safe. It's supposed to go to you when I die, but it'd be better if I gave it to you now. As long as it's clear that I don't want to see you here again, understood? Forget all about this town. If you insist on leaving your family, I'll make sure your husband gets everything. I lowered my gaze and nodded. She gestured towards the door to bid me farewell. Now go with him. I hope we don't have to see each other again.

From the camera's perspective, the composition is shaped like a butterfly spreading its wings: bent knees, toes pointed like wingtips, the opening in the middle awaiting the operation. Someone turns up the music. A cabaret style song plays, Peggy Lee's sugary voice. Gertrudis squeezes the hand of the man who's there as her witness and they look at each other before it begins. He tries to calm her, murmurs a few words in her ear, strokes her forehead and smiles. He goes over to one of the arched windows, hands in the pockets of his tweed suit. Nervous, he watches a fly headbutting the glass. The other man, the photographer, has his head hidden under the curtain of the bellows camera. He presses the shutter and the magnesium powder flashes on the plate. The doctor takes his position in front of the opening. He starts to pull apart the two halves of the speculum so he can insert the dilator, the Pozzi forceps, and then a curette with a six-millimetre handle, an eight-millimetre handle, a twelve-millimetre handle. He sweeps the cavity carefully until he hears the tell-tale sound, also known as a scream, accompanied by a rough texture that indicates the material has been completely removed. The procedure lasts a little over a minute. A dark torrent flows over the edge of the table, drips into the basin designed for that purpose and stains the newspapers spread over the parquet floor. The doctor then removes the gauze and wraps the instruments in linen rags so he can tuck them away into his leather bag.

The pain finally eased on the third day. I'd spent the whole weekend between the bed and the toilet. Luckily, the second-floor bathroom was ready: it had been freshly cleaned and painted – white tiles halfway up the walls and a bright blue above them, like a Zacatecas sky; the tiles and the floor were newly polished, the fixtures replaced. Every few hours I took refuge in warm water, which drained away with the threads of the skein unravelling inside me. I drank electrolyte drinks and took the pills with a sandwich or a couple of biscuits, only to sink back into a deep, blind sleep. On Monday I woke with the sun high in the sky and my stomach rumbling at the smells coming from the kitchen: caramelised onion and garlic, ripe tomatoes, meat softening in steam.

When I emerged, I was surprised by how spacious the hallway looked, and the double height living room conquered by light; an empty space, like a sheet of paper. I heard voices downstairs and went in search of the smell and the cheerful chatter. Oralia's shawl was hanging by the garden door, and before long I spotted her wide back and grey hair plaited with ribbons. She was stirring the contents of a pot on the stove while Mario chopped a bunch of coriander on the table.

'Morning,' I said shyly.

'Morning? It's lunch time!' Doña Oralia rebuked me good-naturedly.

'How are you feeling?' Mario asked. I'd told him I had a stomach bug.

'Better now, I think, thank you. It smells delicious, I'm starving.'

'Go on then, call Lico and the kids to come and wash their hands, food's ready.'

Lico was in the attic. He'd finished restoring the parquet. The children were playing on the little terrace. Come and wash your faces, I said, when I saw them all spattered with white paint. They laughed and said no. We're Apaches, the girl explained, painting two white stripes on her brother's cheeks. What about your feathers? I asked. The Apaches wear a feather crest on their heads. While Lico finished cleaning up and putting away his materials, I cut some leaves from the tulip tree and we stuck them with masking tape onto strips of newspaper, then wound them round our heads. We went to wash our hands, laughing, flicking water at each other, and ran down the stairs, letting out an intermittent war cry with the palms of our hands against our mouths.

The children carried on running around the living room. I plugged in the turntable and put a Teen Tops record on, and we danced to 'mi amor entero es de mi novia Popotitos' until Oralia called for me to take the plates in. Here's fine, we'll fit, she said, and we squeezed around the convent table. In the middle there was queso de rancho, avocado, salsa. Lico was showing the kids how to roll up tortillas: he spread one over his palm, folded one edge over itself and in a single quick slide rolled it into a compact cylinder which he proceeded to sink his teeth into. The children tried to copy him, but their hands were still very little and they laughed at each other's clumsiness. Oralia served bowls of steaming broth with a rich aroma of meat and vegetables. Yum, a proper corpse reviver, I cried when she set the first bowl in front of me, and she let out a laugh. Did you hear? she asked her grandson. She called it a corpse reviver. They both guffawed, and I joined in, though I didn't get the joke. Everyone sat down at the table.

'Aren't you going to eat with us?' I asked Mario when I saw the empty space in front of him.

'He can't,' Oralia said, 'he'd better be hungry when he gets home or his wife will have it in for him.'

Mario nodded, smiling, his hands hidden under the table.

'You should get going, son, it's almost time. Don't forget tomorrow's the last day of the novena.'

Mario stood, kissed his grandmother's hair and said his goodbyes, telling us to tuck in.

'What will you do when you finish here?' I asked Lico.

He chewed slowly, taking his time to reply.

'I think we'll head to the other side. My wife and other children are over there. I'll have to see if we've earned enough to pay for the trip.'

'What about you, Doña Oralia?'

'Oh no, I don't want to cross over. I went once and they sent me back.'

'Really?'

'It was a disaster. I'd rather not think about it.'

'I meant more whether you plan to stay here in the house when we've finished.'

'Oh, well, that depends…' I thought she'd go on, but she fell silent. After a long pause, she asked, 'What about you, child, what will you do?'

'I don't know. I think I'd like to go and see my dad,' I heard myself say, and it was as if the idea had popped right into my mouth; it hadn't even occurred to me before. 'I might work up there for a couple of months, see if I can finally finish my thesis.'

Doña Oralia cut a slice of avocado and offered it to me, the flesh still clinging to the strip of peel. It was perfectly ripe.

'This one's from my hometown,' she said. 'Speaking of which, the little tree you asked me for is outside.'

'Ah, thank you so much! I'll plant it today.'

'Just be quick about it, it'll be dark before long.'

She'd crossed the border in the boot of a car, eighty-four degrees in the shade. From Houston, she took a bus to New York. Not stopping to rest, she ate what she could find at truck stops, carried on to Hartford, found Trinity Academy, took shelter in an alley for several days and wandered the campus until she saw them emerge, more identical than ever, accompanied by some twenty other girls, all taller and blonder than they. She followed the group. They walked two-by-two to the banks of the South Brook River, where they scattered to picnic and play in the grass. She crept closer, her face weary, plaited hair unruly, voice cracked with thirst. She called out to María, who clutched her in a hungry hug when she recognised her and let out a shriek of joy. She asked the girl to lower her voice: no one could know she'd come to bring them back to their mother. She asked María to get her sister and drift off without calling attention to themselves. The blood throbbed in her veins from fear and exhaustion. The twins separated discreetly from the crowd and made their way over to her. But Silvia halted a few steps away. María was untroubled by her nanny's deteri- orated appearance and threw her arms around her waist again without a care in the world. But Silvia took a step back. The woman motioned her to come closer, to trust in her so they could escape. But the twin took another step away, glanced over her shoulder in search of one of the adults in charge. Oralia called out to her: We're going back to your mummy, she said, don't you want to see your mummy? Silvia took a third step and yelled, Miss Betty! Oralia tried to run, but María clung to her with both arms, didn't want to let go. Miss Betty! shouted Silvia, shrilly now. Oralia felt her knees weaken at the sight of the slim blonde governess approaching. She was going to make one last attempt to flee when Miss Betty's pale blue eyes caught her like eagle claws. The incident caused a great uproar all over the county, where nothing ever happened. The police arrested Oralia, locked her up in the local jail and interrogated her, once the interpreter deigned to show up. Her account didn't do much to help her case. The girls' father arrived at the police station around eleven in the morning. He looked at the woman behind the one-way mirror and declared in clear, steady English that he didn't know her, had never seen her before and had no relationship to her, direct or otherwise. He had no idea why she could have tried to kidnap his daughters, and he was willing to press charges, although the judicial process would have to continue in Mexico, where both were citizens. The man left everything else to his lawyer and went on his way. The woman spent a couple of nights behind bars until they came for her, led her handcuffed into a police van and headed onto the highway. The journey back was long and hard. They barely gave her anything to eat or drink, and she pissed herself twice as they refused to let her out to use the bathroom. She tried to escape near Beaumont, but they saw her, and one of the officers, the better marksman, fired his gun. The other unleashed a barrage of complaints, irritated at having come all this way for nothing.

Lico was applying the second coat of black paint to the ironwork. As he finished each room, I'd rearrange the furniture and objects, take stock of what could stay and what couldn't, what needed cleaning or repairs. We'd covered the essentials; now it was just a matter of the space coming slowly to life. There was fire and clean water; there was light, there was music; plants were growing on the balconies; vegetables and cheese were kept cool in the fridge. There was a good life to be lived between these walls. But the more I thought about it, the more I wanted to go back to my hometown and visit my father. Maybe the restoration had kindled my homesickness in some hidden, intangible way. It was absurd: after all the effort of making the house habitable, now I was strangely eager to leave it. Something was unsettling me, destroying me from the inside, an emptiness eating away at its own edges; an egg shell cracking open onto nothing.

I went out to the garden, shovel in hand. The avocado sapling was waiting for me beside the door to the forbidden room, its root wrapped in a black plastic bag. I tried to calculate the distance between the walls and the enclosing garden wall and locate the exact spot where I'd planted the tree in my dream. The hole was less than a foot deep when I knelt and stuck my hands in to dislodge the rounded shape of a biscuit tin, rusted despite being wrapped in a sack, heavy as a meteorite and full of gold bullion coins. Tucked among them was a small velvet bag containing a handful of jewels: a diamond choker, a pair of mother-of-pearl earrings, a ribbon strung with a dozen gold bands. I was so astonished that I took one without thinking, the simplest, set with a red stone, and slipped it on.

I heard the creak of the gate and straightened up with alarm. It took me three seconds to put the lid back on the tin, fold the mouth of the sack, mask my discovery with a bit of earth and cover it by setting the avocado sapling in the hole, plastic bag and all. I brushed the soil off myself and went to meet Zuri, who I could hear calling my name at the entrance. Can you help me, please? There was a car parked outside the house and the boot was crammed with photography supplies, poles, tripods, lamps and cases. We took the things up to the attic and the car drove off. Zuri was surprised to find the space renovated, the beams free of cobwebs, the windows clean, the parquet freshly polished. Lico and I had taken care to collect everything and cover it in plastic so we could fix up one end of the attic, and once we'd finished we moved everything again so he could work on the other side. Now all we had to do was return things more or less to where they'd been: trunk, ottoman, camera cases, screen, props, shelves, boxes.

Zuri took it all in with his hands on his hips, as if he'd been slaving away himself and could finally appreciate the fruits of his labours. He let out a deep sigh. There's a lot of work to do, he said. Then he picked up one of the light stands from the floor and started assembling it with clumsy hands. I've been invited to do a series, he said.

They want everything in analogue. He moved around the attic, unpacking the cameras, opening all the cases. Six images based on a novel, for the fiftieth anniversary of its publication or something like that. The author was friends with my uncle, they were schoolmates. My uncle was working on it when he fell ill and they got in touch to see if I could do it instead. They pay pretty well – Zuri was adjusting the head of a lamp with a butterfly bolt – but I'm short on time, they want the prints the day after tomorrow, it's insane. The bolt slipped out of his trembling hands and skittered onto the floor. I knelt to pick it up. I was thinking maybe you could help me by posing… I felt the heft of the metal in the palm of my hand. It's just six shots, nothing too complicated.

For the second-to-last photo, you lie me down on the floor, on a bone-coloured blanket. The camera is above me, tied to the rafter with a special hot shoe for overhead shots. It's time to conjure the dignitary, the man of letters, the one who only has to say 'let it be so' for reality to materialise. Or 'let it be done' for the fire to catch. I'm suspended in a pleasant daydream, ignoring everything else, and I have no interest in myself or the present or my fear, all of that is far, far away, so far that the scene looks like a minuscule flea circus inside a glass box the size of an earring. I'd need a magnifying glass to watch. But for now, my focus is on my skin, the tickle of a damp brush tracing signs as if from a grimoire all over my arms, face, legs. I smell the ink. You lift the brush to dip it in the well, tamp it onto the edge and continue. My skin can interpret what you're writing: under my right breast, you draw a first row of letters in the alphabet. I don't think they'll fit, but you find a way to distribute all twenty-six letters over three lines. The x, y and z end up on one side of my navel, which serves as the full stop. You write digits one through nine on my lower belly, and, over my pubis, in smaller letters, the caption *goodbye*. Finally, you write *YES* on my right nipple and *NO* on my left. You let the ink dry. I feel the cold of the liquid as it evaporates, leaving the mix of charcoal and squid melanin on my skin. You move away. I hear the screech of an aluminium ladder and suppose you've climbed up to focus the shot. I feel something touching me all over. It moves from one sign to another, like children learning to read, tracing each letter with their finger. It's like the tickle of a wing. Are you there? I hear you asking from above, almost teasing. The touch intensifies and stops on my right nipple. The dignitary is ready to issue the verdict.

There's a party – more like a soirée. The living room furniture has been pushed up against the walls; here and there, smartly dressed people hold tumblers and long-stemmed glasses, smiling, silent. The guests are still, some seated, some leaning against the furniture, others milling around the dining room table, which is laden with platters of hors d'oeuvres: *bastelle*, *anchoïade*, prosciutto crostini, foie gras, toasted brioche, assorted cheeses – Banon, Brie de Meaux and, of course, Camembert; and wine… Between the fireplace and the dining room, a cellist waits with his bow held stiff over his knee.

Everyone is focused on the man seated in an armchair as he reads aloud, one leg crossed over the other. In his right hand is an Old Fashioned made with gin. His left hand presses open a red-bound book. His voice is slightly nasal, and the rhythm of his recitation is mesmerisingly steady. He takes a sip and continues: 'To understand exactly how much the flesh can bear, can resist, note the effort expended by the Dignitary before he exposes the man's ribs. The victim never screams. Perhaps his senses have been muted by so much pain. The Dignitary retreats and positions himself where he appears in the

photograph. From there, he commands the other execu-
tioners to proceed with the quartering as he wipes his
bloodied hands…'

THREE

RESTORATION

I draw the fifth line, the second-to-last, over the other four. Three yins, split line: it successfully restores what was damaged by the father.

It's the same sea. A sea I've already dreamed of, only now the water is choppier, more turbid. The waves beat against the shore, savagely biting the coast's gentle bread. The darkness looms behind me and I try to outrun it. My body feels heavy and my legs cramp with effort. I don't want to look back, don't want to know how close the shadow is, I'm sure it's right on my heels. I know I'm dead if it catches me. Fear claws at my back. I'm losing strength. I look down: my feet are digging into the floor like roots made of sand. My gasps are lost in the pounding surf. I can't take in enough air to keep running, there isn't enough, I'm suffocating, panting, as a larger wave laps at my feet and I splash through the blanket of water. I see a woman approaching. She walks right past. It's me. I recognise my own face as we cross each other's paths. The woman surrenders to the dark power that pursues me and the horror I feel makes me keep running, even though I know I'm reaching the end. I know I'll have to throw myself into the waves so the sea can swallow me instead.

I've had the sewing machine down in the lounge since early this morning, because I needed more room to spread out the cloth for the curtains. I unroll the Terylene onto the dining room table and cut the length of each window, accounting for the pleats and the distance between the sill and the floor. Dressing the house allows me to connect with a warmer, more maternal side of restoration. It's no longer a question of getting things up and running, but rather of making the space feel homey. Sewing somehow brings me back to my mother's lap, the warm light around her hands. I thread the machine so I can hem the edges. I fold the end of the cloth over itself once, then twice. I press the fold under the foot of the machine and step on the pedal; the belt goes taut, activating the mechanism that brings the needle up and down, slowly at first. The white thread unspools from the bobbin, passes through the compartments, the tension springs, drops down into the eye then enters the cloth; moving in and out, in and out, it stitches a long, straight line. Tap-tap, tap-tap, sounds the concert of metallic parts. I need to focus on the point where the needle threads and stitches along its way up, then down, then forward, then up again. The thread obeys the line of the backstitch, one after another, then another, perfectly identical. Stitch and backstitch alternate in a seemingly perpetual rhythm. The straightness of the line depends on my ability to guide its course. The cloth is held captive by the decisive coupling of the tacking stitch. Tap-tap, tap-tap. The steady croon of the machine dissolves all sense of time, the memory of the moment follows swiftly in its footsteps, the present follows close on its heels and splits into two. A Moebius strip, closed in a loop that never ends, never ends, never ends. Suddenly a syncopated noise jolts me from my trance, a knocking sound coming not from the machine but from the window. On the other side of the glass is a moth, thumping desperately in search of shelter from the darkness menacing outside.

I remember that when Eligio brought me to live here, I liked the idea of learning how to decorate, fixing up each room in a different style, with wallpaper that matched the carpets and furniture. He said I could do whatever I wanted, except in the room at the bottom of the stairs, at the back of the house, which is where he develops his photos and stores his work things. I'm not allowed in there. I can't even take a peek while he's working. He overdoes it, insisting I'm going to ruin his rolls of film, but I'm sure he says this just to spook me. He must be keeping something there he doesn't want me to see. As if I didn't know he's always photographing naked women. And wouldn't it be nice if he were only photographing them. But I no longer care. Let him carry on his filthy business, so long as he leaves me alone. Unless he's hiding something else. I bet I could slip in, now that he's not here, and find out what it is. He wouldn't even notice. He leaves the key hanging from the hook by the door, as if to provoke me, as if part of him wanted me to sneak in and see what he's hiding. I don't think anything I could possibly discover would surprise me. But I'm terrified of the man I live with, and that's why I need to see for myself, to know what he's capable of.

The moth persists. It bumps over and over against the glass, battering its wings. It persists until it finally locates the crack in the broken pane. It alights for a moment on the edge and comes in, flutters all around the living room. Its ocelli roam in search of something. I thought it would be drawn to the warm light of the sewing machine, that I'd have to shoo it away and keep it from dirtying the white Terylene with its wing dust, but as it oscillates it drifts away from the glow. It travels to the front hall, circles the coat rack by the door and fixes its legs to one of the keys. Right on that very key. Doubt flickers in my mind. I let the drape slip down to the foot of the sewing machine and get up, go over to the rack. I lean in to study the insect. Its size and shape are that of an ordinary moth, but its wings are red as sindoor powder, as dried blood. Something, maybe its fragility, spurs me to crush it. I reach out a hand. It'll fly away when it feels me there, I think, but it doesn't move. The dust on its wings is so faint it's barely there. I press my thumb and index finger into pincers, press its crumb-light body into the head of the key, squash its skeleton under my fingertip. It beats its wings in a final flail of life, and the redness seeps into the cracks in the metal, in the relief of the word Yale, suffuses the particles of copper and tin, trickles down the toothed shaft. I'm clutching the key in my fist before I even realise what I've done. I feel its weight. There's no turning back now. Key and red are one and the same: they open.

La Castañeda Insane Asylum was a branch of hell on earth. Oralia went every Friday with her basket. She'd bring food, bathe her, drape her in a clean dressing gown and massage her frigid feet, although by the second month the señora was already in a world of her own. There were many cases like hers. Asylums were lawless jails where women were sent for any reason and none. If they weren't already ill, they were sickened with horse tranquilisers and electroshock therapy. Oralia would sit on a bench in the courtyard, and as she waited for them to bring her out, all kinds of lunatics would come to sit beside her; both men and women, but more often women, who'd start chatting out of nowhere: I wanted to go back to Sinaloa to see Mami, and, well, I up and borrowed my husband's car cause I didn't have the money for the bus. They caught me on the way and brought me here, but they're just trying to scare me, I'm sure my husband will come get me tomorrow and take me home / They all left: my first husband, my daughter who got married at fifteen, my other daughter who took a bunch of pills and that was her gone too, my second husband, my son. Everyone leaves and then you're on your own,

what did they expect me to do after they left me alone /
He's so stupid, stupid, stupid. It was his fault, not mine /
A mother needs to be with her son, she needs to watch
him grow up, she needs to take care of him. A son needs
to be with his mother, or else he falls prey to his vices.
My son already had lots of vices, that's why I had to kill
him / I worked all the time, had ten, fifteen men every
day. But there's no way around getting old. One night
when I'd had a few too many I woke up in the stairwell,
stiff as an ice lolly. Sometimes a girl loses her head and
can't remember anything. I walked in here on my own
two feet because I knew I had nothing left out there and
there had to be something in here, even just a cup of hot
atole / Did you find them, Oralia? Did you go and get
them? Please go and get them, Oralia, I'm begging you.
I'll give you whatever you want, just please save them, for
the love of God, take them far away to your village where
he can't find them. Please, please. Please. Kill him if you
have to. That's why I had the knife with me. He needs
to die, Oralia. You have to kill him. He'll kill us all if you
don't kill him. I have to tell you something. It's a secret,
it's a terrible thing, but I can't talk right now. The words
won't come out. Come back tomorrow and I'll tell you.
Won't you go and get the girls tomorrow? I can give
you lots of gold. Tons of gold, just promise me you'll take
care of them, take them to the park, buy them ice cream,
and buy yourself whatever you want, Oralia. Come back
tomorrow and I'll tell you where it is. Just don't breathe
a word to him. Promise me you won't. Promise me you'll
go and get the girls, Oralia. Promise me you'll bury the
knife in that monster. He won't stop unless you kill him
/ Sometimes a girl loses her head.

I'm the one who goes. Clutching the key in my fist. I'm the movement compelling the sole of the foot into the wind, the will to know, the impatient urge to sink the toothed edge into the lock, the yen to give it a turn or two and open the door. It's me who delves into the darkness to see what's inside. For an instant, I'm christened with another name. Curiosity, I'm called. I inhabit the woman's form. I'm what drives her forwards. She, in turn, makes my insides pulse. I've already made her cross the threshold between the living room and the dinette, between the dinette and the kitchen, which is sunken – lights out at this hour – in a nearly nocturnal leadwort-blue. She moves through the shadows cast by the furniture. I place her hand on the handle of the mosquito screen to the garden, and she pushes it, fluttering the cool fragrance of the herbs growing in the garden: rue, rosemary, basil. I'm the eye that dwells beyond consciousness. An eye that knows ahead of time, that imagines and yearns to discover the best and the worst, the unexpected, the terrible. I conjecture what lies beneath the lid of the trunk, of the box, on the other side of the door, behind the heavy black curtains. I can see through the binding of the books, the shutters of the writing desk. If I'm told not to look, I look. If I'm forbidden to turn back, I'm transformed into a pillar of salt. Like the *Condylura cristata*, I use the moist, waxy valves I perceive with to seek out the subtlest trace of horror and surprise. Don't trust anyone, I always tell myself. Once I find the merest glimmer of conjecture, my hunger stirs. The hunger to see, to open, grows inside me like a magic bean. What turns out to be on the other side is the least of it. What I want is to tear the veil. The very instant when what's hidden is revealed – that's what quickens my pulse. Take cats, for example. The cat is my slave. It scratches the box merely to peer into the darkness and the void, hears a faint, surreptitious noise and leaps paws-first into the black hole, which could contain poison just as readily as food. The chase is infinitely more satisfying to us than the flesh of our prey. It's this game that grants meaning to everything else. If I were to disappear, if I were to lose the airs and graces that mark me as a powerful animal, everyone in the world would be lost. But they've got me. I won't fail them. If they feed me, I grow. If they ignore me, I punish them, sticking their bodies with pins. I make my way along the path towards the hidden face of the house. Towards the door to the forbidden room. I feel it strengthen and expand, the impulse that inhabits and dominates me, that assails me with uncertainties as if they were snowballs. I'm the instant before. The assumption. Before I open the door, I imagine the best and the worst: the treasure and the axe plunged deep into a stump. The revelation of love and the floor drenched in blood. Epiphany and death. It's very rare that what I find is even more horrific than what the imagination can conjure.

For the last photograph, there's a tripod in the middle of the attic, an easel whose legs have been secured to the parquet. I'm going to be mounted on it like a painting. They'll make a painting of my body. They lift my weight and rest my back against the crossed poles. My crossed arms, tied behind me, tense. I can see myself reflected in the lens: five points, the ideogram for the number six, the starfish. The tripod takes my weight and wrests the heads of my humerus bones from their joints, tearing the ligaments. My clavicles creak like branches, as if a lightning bolt had cleaved the tulip tree in two, clawing it open from on high. They talk; they listen to music and talk amongst themselves. The eldest gives instructions. The youngest snaps away at whim with the Hasselblad, the Nikon, focuses the Pascal, rewinds the film in the manual cameras and shoots. It's not my best angle, although my straining torso must look svelte. The dignitary delivers his statement, then waits, hands in his pockets, to take his place in the photograph. Now it's the eldest who takes on the role of the doctor. He dons the white coat, grips the blade. He draws the steel over the skin, careful not to cause any more damage than intended. The damage must be precise, restrained enough for the captive to stay alive. Otherwise, it'll lose all artistic merit and succumb to vulgarity, to the butcher's vehemence. In this sense, it's not a matter of being gratuitously violent, but of exercising this harm with a delicacy befitting a surgeon or a painter, a musician skilled in playing the strings and studiedly slicing the bow. Once he's traced red circles around my breasts, as if he'd employed a fine brush dipped in red paint instead of a scalpel, he proceeds to wrest with the purposefulness of someone harvesting fruit. One might picture the act of extirpation causing a natural flow of blood. In truth, though, the procedure was executed with such dexterity that the bleeding barely escapes the surgical cut, trickling in two slender lines down toward the inner thighs. Clusters of ganglia slip through his gloved fingers, the lymph oozes, fatty tissue quivers in the two morbid bulbs that the man places in the canopic vase: the blue porcelain vessel set on the shelf, beside the dead flowers.

The interdiction echoes in the dark like a voice in a dream. You may open all the doors of the castle except that one. And so, if you should open it, my rage will know no limits. It isn't something I hear, it's something I know. It throbs in the shadows, because it was here long before I arrived, long before I parted the curtain, before I slid the bolt across and opened the door, before I fit the toothed edge into the lock, before I took a chance, before I crushed the fragile red body of the moth into the head of the key. I'm her, the doubting woman. It's her touch that finds the switch and flicks it. A tenuous glow bleeds into the limits of the walls. The hermetic room is the same size I'd calculated from outside, though it seems smaller in the darkness that coats the walls and ceiling. The light doesn't illuminate, but rather engulfs, subjects the gaze to the empire of its redness: the stained sink, red, the plastic drums and funnels, red, the shelves, the night-stand, the pewter basins, all red, the developing liquid, red, red on red and red, a four-walled ventricle flooded with scarlet. She moves past the enlarger and the cutting table and heads straight for the board hanging on the back wall. There, pinned up, lit by the red transparency of the safelight, she finds a set of shapes captured in time. Plays of light and shadow captured in fine layers of emulsion spread over paper fibres. Features and shapes that are the synecdoche of an unquestionable reality: a woman quartered on a tripod, a bloody open-winged butterfly, two eleven- or twelve-year-old girls, identical, horrendously beautiful, whose bodies are displayed with a most unchildlike intent. At first I refuse to recognise them, but I see their hair and my hands feel the texture I know from combing it so many times; I see the lace of their white camisoles and remember sewing it myself; I see their faces and identify the minute differences that let me know which brow I'm kissing. Then I understand what the photo suggests and the revelation strikes me in the back of the neck like an axe. Sometimes a girl loses her head.

I have no idea how long I've been here. I know I did things, beat the air furiously, shouted insults, brandished my hatred. I know they punished my waylaid body outside, that they shaved my head, that I rotted in my own filth and they tossed my carcass into a mass grave. But in truth, ever since the dark came down around me, I haven't been able to leave this place. I can't move, everything is pitch black. The darkness swallowed the world, the stars, the moon, the park, the streetlamps, the buildings, and descended over the house. It's a sea of tar entrapping me. I don't know how long I've been like this, knees pressed to my chest, snared in the pain that gripped me in its talons, caused by a force I can't even remember. Everything is so far away that I no longer know who I am, just that the pain comes at times and claws at me from within, although I can't recall why. Suddenly I hear a noise at the door, the wind blows, the heaviness releases my chest. I grope my way out. It's dark outside, too. All that can survive this dense darkness is the wan glow of embers illuminating the back of an old woman in the garden, knife in hand, cutting handfuls of rue, basil and rosemary. Her head is covered in a mottled shawl.

May wonders never cease, she says, look who decided to come out, and I recognise her voice, but I can't piece her together in my memory, she must be someone I know from long ago. Alright, off with those clothes and get in, the stones are ready. The old woman wraps the herbs into a bundle and murmurs a prayer. I see a hole dug in the centre of the garden and an avocado sapling that someone has begun to plant. But they've left the job half-finished. It's there! I tell the old woman, pointing to the tree, and I feel relieved, free. Come on now, it's getting late: she hurries me along with a wave of her hand. Inside the brick dome is the fire and the water. I take off my dress, bra and knickers. I take the handful of herbs she holds out. She grants me permission. I crawl in on my knees and am received by a warm, womb-like embrace. My heart crumbles like a clod of earth in the rain. Sit down on that rock there, she says. Give the fire a drink to open the first door. I reach out in the darkness and find a pot with a dipping gourd. I pour out the first gourdful onto the scorching pebbles and hear them crackle. The woman speaks in a kind of chant. She says a prayer for me. Steam fills the space. My body turns to tears, to sweat, to liquid; my arms and legs are torrents. Introduce yourself to the fire, tell it your name. I tell her I don't know what my name is. So she says in her prayer that I am presenting myself stripped of a name, and she asks me to pour out the second gourdful of water. It mutters and sizzles, the particles fill the air, I let myself be swept along by the music of her words. Every so often she goes quiet and waits for me to open the next door. She asks me to surrender my hunger, my desolation, my shame. The fire receives and destroys them. My soul embraces the fragrant soul of the basil and rue, I scrub my pain against their fibres. I allow myself to be trawled by the solace of the voice as it puts things in order, restores me to my origin: fear and memory remain here. Pain remains here. Anguish remains and weeping remains, the blood remains, the body remains. The music of her words sinks me into a benevolent sea so powerful that it cleaves the rift I flee through, drawn to a new moon.

My father used to tell children a cruel and stupid joke. He'd tell it as a riddle: Which feels more pain, the dog when you cut off its tail or the tail when you cut off its dog? The answer was the tail. It was the tail that had the most to lose: so too this farewell to feet and calves that are no longer, that are no longer with me, that must be mourning the loss of my body. There's great sorrow in realising that this cell over here will never again accompany that cell over there. Same with the nerves, done firing and connecting: a snapped cable, forsaken, a desolation of muscular fibres forever released. Ligaments, weary of contracting, give up; they've lost the opposing tension that once pulled them taut; the force that pulled them makes the blood flow through the arteries' transversal cut. When the blade pierces the skin, it lightly crushes the soft spot where pressure is applied before sundering the edges that will never re-join. Next, the vulva: the blade enters and the hand pulls at the folds like the petals of a succulent; the organ of pleasure speaks, only to transform the mouth into a rupture, its silence into a river. The heart, however, keeps beating slowly, calmly, as if asleep; it doesn't notice, it's just a dumb muscle pulsing, an automaton that no longer even belongs to me. The sky opens overhead. Sixth line, yang: she serves neither kings nor princes. She withdraws in pursuit of the sublime. The idea of me, the thing I am, ceases to occupy the broad space of flesh, and shrinks; it flinches from pain, retracts into a tiny centre. Escapes the blade. It flees from one organ to the next. It rises from the oesophagus into the throat, the mouth. I can feel the elusive capsule on my tongue like the seed of a fruit. It stirs. The pupa breaks out and is born. Flutters. I open my mouth and it darts out in search of the crack, the fissure in the glass, the pinprick of light.

Memory and oblivion imply each other like a lock and key. We realise we've forgotten, that we're forgetting, as soon as the memory sends forth its lightning bolt. You might be relaxing at home, say, sewing some curtains, without grasping that you've been forgetting something important, something essential, something that no longer exists, that whatever you're looking at is just a mirage. A ghost is a fragment of memory that has forgotten itself. I can travel to and fro along the paths of an invented universe, brew coffee in the morning, bake bread, take a bath, sow my own bones in the ground and eat the fruit borne of my own remains, until I entirely forget the notion of night and day, space and the body. But the circuit closes onto itself, the moth slips in, alights on the key, and I open, see the photograph, and realise what I am. Memory can be recovered. Forgetting cannot.

It's Friday and the sun begins its descent beyond the clouds. An opal light illuminates the main living area, shining on whitewashed walls. Zuri's in the darkroom. He came by to print the photos he needs to deliver tomorrow. The house is ready. Lico finished painting the ironwork inside and out. It's time to pay him. I place three gold coins into his rough palm and he smiles, satisfied. The kids are waiting for him outdoors; I can hear their laughter drifting away. I ask if he was able to replace the weather-head for the cables, but he says no, he hasn't done any electrical work since the system he installed in his own home started the fire that killed him, his wife and his nine children; they all slept crowded together in the same room. He says my father went to the funeral and cried a lot; he'd never attended one with so many or such small coffins. Lico pauses by the enclosing wall and puts on his straw-coloured jacket before he leaves.

Now I know what I have to do.

I return to the hook by the door and remove the red-stained key again. I step out into the garden. Once more, I insert the toothed edge into the lock and turn it three times, now in the opposite direction. I hear the struggle on the other side, the pounding on the door,

Zuri's agitated shouts. Open up, who's there? Aunt Silvia, is that you? Come on, I'm not being funny. Open the door. I move away along the footpath. If there were a lake or ocean nearby, I'd toss the key into the water, but I'll have to settle for the storm drain on the corner.

I cross the street towards Mario's truck and lean against the window on the passenger side. He takes off his headphones. He's listening to the game. I catch a snippet of the rumble in the stadium, the commentator's voice.

'I'm heading out, just came to say goodbye. Thanks for everything.'

He nods and looks through the windshield as if he were driving.

'Did you see her before she left?' he asks sadly. He seems disappointed.

'No.' I shake my head. 'But she asked me to tell you to please finish planting the avocado tree.'

Mario's brow furrows, apprehensive, and he smiles faintly.

'Really?'

'Yeah. Just don't take too long, it'll be dark soon,' I tell him, and I go, my footsteps vanishing down the wooded paths.

CHARCO PRESS

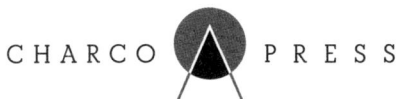

Director & Editor: Carolina Orloff
Director: Samuel McDowell

www.charcopress.com

Restoration was printed on
80gsm Munken Cream paper.

The text was designed using Bembo 11.5 and ITC Galliard.

Printed in April 2025 by Bell and Bain Ltd.
303 Burnfield Road, Thornliebank, Glasgow G46 7UQ
using responsibly sourced paper.